DOMESTICATING THE ALIEN

BEASTLY ALIEN BOSS, BOOK 5

AVA ROSS

DOMESTICATING THE ALIEN

Beastly Alien Boss Series, Book 5

Cover art by Natasha Snow Designs

Editing/Proofreading by JA Wren & Owl Eyes Proofs & Edits

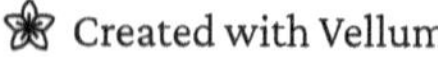 Created with Vellum

FOREWORD

A note to the reader.

If you found this book outside of Amazon,
it's likely a stolen/pirated copy.
Authors make nothing when books are pirated.
If authors are not paid for their work,
they can't afford to keep writing.

*For my parents who
always believed I could do this.*

SERIES BY AVA

Mail-Order Brides of Crakair

Brides of Driegon

Fated Mates of the Ferlaern Warriors

Fated Mates of the Xilan Warriors

Holiday with a Cu'zod Warrior

Galaxy Games

*Alien Warrior Abandoned/
Shattered Galaxies*

Beastly Alien Boss

Bride of the Fae

Stranded With an Alien/A Sci-fi Holiday Tail

Monsterville, USA
(Includes Monster Between the Sheets
& Sweet Monster Treats)

Monster On Board
(Co-written with Alana Khan)

You can find my books on Amazon.

DOMESTICATING THE ALIEN

**I've been hired to teach an alien warrior
social skills to woo a mate.
But now he's trying to woo me.**

When the elderly duchess I cared for dies, her slimy son—my ex—tells me he wants me back. Um, no. I flee to the Intergalactic Employment Agency, where I'm offered a job teaching an alien warlord sophistication so he can woo a mate at the upcoming Match-Mating Soiree. If anyone can domesticate a brute, it's me.

In between coaching Forje on how to converse politely and dance without crushing his partner's tail, he shares his dreams and unusual poetry. He's sweetly cute in a gruff, grumbly way, and it's not long before I see he's awesome even if he doesn't know which fork to use with the main course.

But when we arrive at the Match-Mating Soiree, and alien females cluster around him, I'll lose the guy I've come to adore. Unless I can convince him I'm the one in need of domestication.

Domesticating the Alien is Book 5 in the Beastly Alien Boss Series. Each book is loosely connected and features an Earth woman hired for an off-world job who meets a gruff alien who can't resist falling for his fated mate.

CHAPTER ONE
KALEI

"Ashes to ashes, dust to dust," the Reverend said solemnly, his rheumy gaze hitching across the small group of people gathered around the grave. "We therefore commit our dearly beloved Duchess Viola to the ground. May she rest in the arms of the heavens above."

Dressed in black, I stood in the drizzling rain mourning my former mother-in-law, Viola's, loss. As far as I could tell, I was the only one upset that she'd died. She'd been old. She'd had cancer. And she was estranged from her son, my ex-husband. It wasn't much of a surprise that so few had turned up to say goodbye.

I'd lived with her, helping her during her final days, but she'd survived longer than expected, eighteen months, actually. She'd passed a week ago, and I'd made the funeral arrangements and notified my ex, Rich, who she hadn't spoken to since he and I split.

I missed her. She'd been strict, and while she'd been a stickler for protocol and insisted I serve all her meals as if she dined with a king, I'd loved her.

I sniffed.

The weight of someone's gaze fell on me from across the grave, and I looked up, cringing to see Rich standing there. Tall and thin, he was older than me. When had he started graying at the temples? He watched me down his hawkish nose, and his expression wasn't pleasant. Actually, it was creepy, as if he was undressing me while I stood beside my friend's grave. Not just my friend. His *mother*.

How sick. The sooner her service was over, the quicker I could return to my small apartment at Viola's estate and continue packing. I wasn't sure what would happen with her estate, but she no longer needed me. I'd move into a hotel room until I found a new job. Surely, I'd be qualified for other caregiver positions. Viola gave me a reference not long ago.

It seemed like tending to dying women was my role in life. After I cared for my aunt, who'd raised me, I'd married Rich. When we divorced, and he stalked me, she'd stepped in and told him to behave. Then she asked me to live with her and assist her with her vast estate.

She'd been stuffy and stilted and . . . my eyes welled with tears again. I'd cried on and off since she stopped breathing, missing her kindness and wry sense of humor. Missing the protection she'd provided against Rich. She only had to speak to him once, and he left me alone.

The Reverend's gaze swept across us again, and I realized he was finished. "Thank you for coming today. I know the Duchess would be pleased."

I wasn't sure about that. If asked today, her lips would twist, and she'd tell me this was what happened when a person isolated themselves from life.

On her deathbed, she made me promise to do something spontaneous. Did ordering my coffee with almond milk instead of cream count as spontaneity? It hardly mattered now. I'd taken her advice to heart, however, and I was determined to step out of the mold I'd made for myself when I first moved in with my elderly aunt at the age of fourteen.

Leaving the grave, I walked back to the parking lot, avoiding puddles. I lifted my wrist com, to hail a shuttle to take me back to the estate, and it didn't take long to arrive.

It landed in front of me, and the hatch opened. Inside, I stared through the plexiscreen as the shuttle lifted off and zipped above the city, landing on the paved driveway in front of Viola's estate.

I went inside, but before I could hurry to my room, Rich opened the front door and stepped into the foyer.

"Why are you here?" I asked, my spine twitching.

"This is my home now." His head dipped forward, and his lips twitched with a sly smile.

Why had it taken me so long to see through his slick charm? I was naïve, I suppose.

No longer.

"If you'll be so kind as to come with me to the parlor," he said, striding that way. "We need to talk."

With a shrug, I followed. It wouldn't take long to pack the rest of my things and call for transport. It was time for me to find a new—no, *spontaneous*—place in the world. I'd make sure it was as far from Rich as possible.

"My mother left everything to me in her will," he said, perching on the edge of one of the flower-patterned chairs. He waved to another nearby. "I have a proposition for you."

"What is it?" I'd listen, but I doubted he'd offer anything of any value.

The memory of Viola's smile ripped through me, making it hard to breathe. My eyes stung with tears, but I'd cried enough this past week. It was time to move forward and seek the life she'd encouraged me to find.

"Since you are now without employment," he said grandly, "you are welcome to remain here . . . with me."

From the slimy look in his eyes, it wasn't hard to guess what he was offering. I stood. "No, thanks." Never again.

"My mother is no longer here to protect you. You. Are. Mine."

"I'm not," I gasped, rising and backing to the doorway. "You can't do this to me." I'd go to the police and—

I'd gone to the police when he first threatened me, but they hadn't done much. It was only when Viola spoke to him that he backed down and left me alone.

He stood, a slick grin rising on his face. "I'm the duke, and you are my wife."

"The divorce was finalized two years ago." I'd made sure of that.

"In my mind, you are still mine. My mother is no longer here to . . . command me."

Forget being his. It was time to get spontaneous. Turning, I fled. But when I started down the hall to go to my rooms, where I'd grab a few things and run, he stalked after me, his hands outstretched.

Fear blasted through me. I veered to the right and raced down the hall, bursting through the back door. I crept close to the shrubs, making my way toward the front of the enormous building. In no time, I was jogging down the driveway and out onto the main road with no possessions other than the small clutch in my hand.

Bangs rang out behind me, telling me Rich wasn't giving up yet.

I hurried along the sidewalk, grateful when I reached the main part of town without Viola's son catching up.

What was I going to do? I had my purse and my com, so I could access my bank credits, but I'd left everything I owned back at Duchess Viola's estate. Maybe I could hire someone to collect them for me.

Until then, it would be a good idea to get out of town fast.

A sign hanging from the building ahead drew my eye. *Intergalactic Employment Agency.*

Intergalactic, huh? If I could find an off-world job, I could leave Earth and never return. Who cared about old clothing? Since my room was small, I kept my favorite pictures of my aunt and Viola on my com. I didn't *need* anything at the estate.

I rushed inside the agency, the bell overhead jangling, and turned to peer through the plexi. No Rich in sight, so far.

"Welcome to the Intergalactic Employment Agency," someone said in a chipper voice behind me. "Where your employment dreams come true."

The sales pitch sounded like overkill, but I assumed they were required to spit out the line to anyone walking through the front door.

I turned to find an alien striding toward me, his hand outstretched. "I'm Quengron, but you may call me Quen. What sort of position are you seeking?"

"Something off-world. I need a job fast."

The gray, segmented skin on his brow scrunched, though his solitary eye sparkled. "This is the norm lately."

"What do you mean?"

"In recent days, we've sent employees to various planets within moments of their hire. And some actually end up mating with their bosses, though I will point out that we are not a matchmating service."

Ugh. "I'm not looking for anything like that."

"They said that as well." His fangs flashed with his smile. "Why don't you allow me to access your com, and we'll see what you're qualified for? We can discuss options after that."

"All right." I held up my wrist, and he scanned it with the dash—a small, hovering computer.

He studied the data on his side of the device. "Ah, yes, I see that you have experience caring for our dearly departed."

"I took care of my aunt and Duchess Viola."

"Duchess?"

"Yes, she was literally a Duchess, a title bestowed on her family by a queen many generations ago. Her son . . ." It might be best not to mention him. "I did more for Duchess Viola than just care for her during her final days. When she was still vigorous, I was her assistant. I scheduled social engagements for her, plus arranged various events. She was a stickler for protocol and social graces, and I learned a lot during her employ."

"Ah, I see." Quen said, rounding the plexi counter at the back of the room, his dash zipping behind him. "We can offer you a few positions that might suit. The first is on the Vivaton Space Station in the Segular Quadrant."

"What does the job entail?"

"Someone is seeking a person to care for his two orphaned yarlings." He frowned at the screen.

"A single dad, huh?"

"It says here that the yarlings are . . . challenging, and he would like to employ someone who is capable of providing them with an education, plus taming them, if possible. This is why I'm suggesting this job to you. It is similar to your prior position, is it not?"

Not in the least. I liked kids, but . . . "I don't believe I'm suited to look after children." Let alone tame them. "I've never done anything like that before."

"I see." He squinted at the screen. "Very well, then. The second position is with the Faraley royal family."

A spark lit inside me, and I rushed over to the counter, leaning across it. "Tell me more."

"The king is seeking someone to care for his queen."

This job sounded better. "What would this position entail?"

He sniffed, and a frown filled his face. "Do you know the Faraley species at all?"

Oh-oh. "I don't. Tell me about them."

"They are multi-limbed and excrete a liquid that can be quite caustic, though I'm sure they would provide you with the proper equipment to ensure your human skin is not burned too badly."

I winced and rubbed the exposed flesh on my arms. "I'm not sure about this."

"We've had a hard time filling this position. It comes with a generous bonus, and I'm quite confident you won't find her odor too repulsive."

"That isn't the right job for me. Do you have any other job openings?"

He studied the dash screen again. "Ah, here is one I haven't seen before. Someone is seeking a person to teach a Haehron warlord proper social skills."

"Why, so I can mate with him?" I wasn't sure where my sharp mouth came from. Maybe because shouts were ringing out on the street, and I worried Rich had already located me.

"Actually, mating will not be required for this position. It states here that he would like to learn the appropriate behavior needed so he can find a mate at the Match-Mating Soiree."

I inched over to the right wall, pressing my back against it to give me a good view of the street while still able to see Quen. "I haven't heard of the soiree, but this job sounds good. Tell me more."

"You will teach him dance, social etiquette, polite conversation, plus accompany him to the soiree and guide him as needed while he selects a mate."

"It sounds perfect." Beyond my dreams, actually. "There's only one problem. You said he's of a different species. I don't understand Haehron dance or etiquette."

"His family states they will explain things as necessary."

Okay, so maybe they behaved similarly to humans.

"I'll take the job," I said. Shouts outside grew louder. I inched closer to Quen. "Can I leave now?"

"Of course," he said. "Because so many new hires are demanding immediate employment, we've opted to put together a bag of items you may take with you." He held up his com. "If you would be so kind as to step away from the wall so I can scan you, the fabricator will craft appropriate clothing for your new position. Just a few outfits, however. You'll be expected to obtain others once you arrive, but this position comes with a generous clothing allowance, likely due to the events surrounding the soiree."

"Awesome." I held my arms out from my sides while his com scanned me. A ding sounded behind him, and he opened the fabricator and removed several items, placing them into a nylatek bag.

"Your shuttle will be here—"

A bang, and it landed in the chute to his right. The hatch opened.

"Well, well," he said with a grin. "When we say right away, we deliver, do we not?"

Someone banged on the front door.

"Well, I've never . . ." the clerk said, hurrying around the counter.

I snatched the bag from his hand as he passed and hopped into the shuttle. The hatch closed, and the sickly-sweet scent of gas filled the chamber.

The last thing I saw as stasis engulfed me was Rich stomping through the front door.

"It's over," I shouted. "You'll never find me now."

A snarl ripped from him. "There is no corner of the galaxy you can run to where I won't find you."

CHAPTER TWO
FORJE

I stood with my squadron in the neutral zone between the Haehron colony wall and the land appropriated by the Twarvians.

As the leader of my squadron in the Haehron military, it wasn't the norm for me to participate in skirmishes like this, but I needed to keep my skills honed. Battling Twarvians eager to reach the wall encircling our large colony also provided great exercise.

As a pack of Twarvians oozed closer, I tightened my grip on the sword in my left hand and zapper in my right.

When one of the endangered species and its egg sack were located on a space station in the Treskar quadrant, they were transported here in the hopes that they'd prosper. It was believed they'd originated on the planet Tooline, which was destroyed when a large meteor hit it.

Unfortunately for my colony, the creatures had thrived too well on this planet. Now, the oozing translucent gray blobs were no longer endangered. In fact, there was risk they would put me and my fellow Haehrons on the endangered list instead.

The Twarvians, creatures at least twice my size and with voracious appetites, shifted closer across the rocky ground. They sought easy prey, which would not be us. Their numerous spiked tentacles waved in the air. As tempting as it would be to slice off their limbs, we'd discovered that was the second way they multiplied; each limb grew into another Twarvian. They also mated and laid egg sacks, which we destroyed during regular patrols to keep them from overrunning us.

"Attack," I snarled, stomping forward. If we didn't start battling, my mind would wander and . . .

The exact lines of poetry I'd been trying to come up with as we started our patrol came to me.

She is mist in the air.

Her lips golden and ripe,

like the crust of the most luscious stavia bread.

My second-in-command, Krevair, rushed beside me with his zapper lifted, his shrieking battle cry centering my mind on the coming fight.

Now that they were no longer nearing extinction, we were allowed to kill those who threatened the colony.

The trick was to spark the Twarvians with the zapper, then plunge my sword between any of the eyeballs. I needed to drive it deeply and twist within the brains before the creature had the chance to bite me with its fangs— which would immobilize me long enough for it to engulf me. If that happened, I'd struggle in its belly while it slowly consumed me.

Not this dia.

My hearts clenched at the thought of the friends I'd lost before we figured out how to control the Twarvian numbers and keep them from swarming the colony.

The pack of Twarvians shrieked en masse, their five

eyeballs locking on us. Their oozing pace increased, and they slithered our way. I counted at least twenty, a solid challenge for the five males in my squadron.

We drew closer, and I leaped, soaring over the lead Twarvian. As I passed above the creature, its tentacled limbs snapped out, trying to grab me. I twisted as I plunged toward the ground, slamming my blade between the third and fourth eyeballs. Falling, I added my weight, pressing my blade into its brain.

The creature flopped on the ground, dead.

Krevair and my other squadron males did the same, quickly dispatching the rest. A few slithered toward the endless rolling hills where they resided, but we didn't give chase. They'd tell their larger pack what happened here, and we'd remain safe from attack for a few dias. By then, their hunger would grow to the point they'd be eager to attempt the wall encircling the colony once again.

It was a sad ongoing mission, though my commanding officers recently told me there may be a solution.

"Well done," I told my friends, nudging the Twarvian I'd dispatched with my boot. When it didn't move, my spine loosened.

As I grinned at my fellow Haehrons, the sense of pride I felt would stay with me for dias. There were no other males I'd rather battle with than these.

The Twarvian by Krevair's feet shifted, and its limbs snapped out to encircle his waist and legs. It scrambled toward the hills, desperate to escape long enough to engulf my friend. Krevair's fangs snapped together, and he grunted as he squirmed and stabbed the creature with his sword.

I wasn't sure where his zapper was.

With a bellow, I raced after them. I slammed my blade

between its eyes and gave it a vicious twist. The creature flopped, releasing Krevair.

My pulse thundered as I helped him to his feet, checking him over quickly to ensure he wasn't wounded.

"You are all right?" I asked.

"My mate is going to kill me," he mumbled, gently assessing his nose that bloomed with color already. Its crooked slant told me it was broken. "We are supposed to attend the Match-Mating Soiree with our eldest son in a few dias, and now my nose will be twice its normal size."

"Let me fix it."

"I appreciate the offer, but my mate will see to me." Wincing, he shook his head, his silver hair shifting along his back. "At least we have a break coming up."

We were both off for ten dias.

"I'll walk back with you to the station, then," I said.

We joined the others and left the open neutral zone, heading toward the enormous wall encircling the colony. We kept the zone around the wall clear of brush and debris, and the clean-up crew would come out later to burn the bodies.

Like during most of my free time, my mind spun away, swallowed by the poems I created for myself alone. I rarely put them to paper, partly because they were never quite good enough, but mostly because . . .

They were awful. So others said when I shared. I enjoyed composing them, however. How else could a male occupy his mind during a long patrol?

She walks with a sturdy gait.

Majestic and pure.

All hear her coming.

And my hearts thundered . . .

I frowned. How would my hearts respond to a lovely

female's arrival? I also wasn't sure why I so often composed poems about females. After Shardeene rejected me, I should create poems about battle. Still, my mind kept returning to females.

My hearts thundered . . .

With dismay— No, no, that sentiment might be true, since I had no interest in mating after what happened with Shardeene, but for a poem, one could not state they greeted a female with dismay. They'd meet her with . . . joy. Yes, that worked well.

My hearts thundered with joy and . . .

Snarling behind me sent me spinning, my weapons lifting. A Twarvian we'd missed arched itself toward me. Bellowing, I raced toward it, swinging my zapper in its direction, hitting its underside chest with the tip. I engaged the weapon, sending arcs through the creature, stunning it.

While the other males gathered around us, ready to jump in if I had need, the beast squealed, its tentacled limbs smacking my legs. I plunged my sword between its eyes, killing the struggling creature, then stood over it, panting.

"You're bleeding," Krevair said, nudging his chin toward my face. A swipe of my scarred hand revealed he was right.

"It is nothing," I said.

He grunted and turned back to the stone gate. Males patrolling the top of the wall had stopped, and their gazes were fixed on us.

My attention was caught by something at the top of a distant hill, and I swore it was a skimmer, but who'd travel that far from the colony? Twarvians oozed and slithered.

Only *Vessars* might be so bold. They lived far from here, but . . . Had the lizard mafia decided to venture close to the colony? I'd notify my supervisors just in case.

"Coming?" Krevair asked, his gaze following mine. "Do you see something?"

I squinted in that direction, but nothing moved. I shrugged. "Maybe not."

He nodded and turned back to the others.

With unease settling into my bones, I trudged behind them, keeping my ears tuned for subtle sounds that would indicate attacking Twarvians. Or Vessars, for that matter.

After a long patrol, my muscles ached. Killing wore out my body. But we couldn't let the Twarvians invade the colony.

Where was I with my poem? I'd left off at . . . *The shrill cry of a . . .*

We reached the gate and waited for it to grind open before trudging inside, our boots stirring the soil, our souls heavy.

For the next line of my poem, I needed the exact word, one that would fit the beauty of the one I dreamed of. I did not expect to meet her in reality, and if I did, I wasn't sure what I would do with her.

Her voice is the shrill cry of a layderstork.

As the gate shut behind us, we walked over to our skimmers. While they couldn't be driven off-planet, they were perfect for local hover travel.

"See you in ten dias?" Krevair said, slapping my shoulder.

I settled my weapons in the back of my skimmer. "Yes."

Ten dias until I was needed to lead my squadron again. What was I going to do with my free time?

"Enjoy yourself at the Match-Mating Soiree," I told him.

He grinned, wincing when the gesture shifted his nose. "Let us hope my son settles on a mate. Aerista is eager for grandyarlings."

I braced his arms. "I hope your dwelling is soon overrun with them."

"That would be nice." He fed me a sappy smile, telling me his mate was not the only one excited about grandyarlings.

As he strode to his own skimmer, I settled inside mine. I engaged the engine and lifted it off the ground, sending it soaring above the tree line, toward the center of our town where I'd planted and cultivated my wellire dwelling. My aunties had soon settled with me at the colony, and despite the Twarvians, we enjoyed this planet. Our home planet's sun had faded to the point the land no longer had seasons other than cold. This planet gave us shelter and a new place to call home.

I landed my skimmer in the holding area on the edge of town and opened the hatch.

"Forje," a high-pitched voice cried from the main street ahead. I smiled as one of my two aunties gestured for me to approach them. "We must speak with you this instant."

"Later, Aunties?" I asked. Tired, I only wished to reach our dwelling where I would strip, bathe my weary body, and collapse on my bed. I'd sleep for three dias.

Since I loved my aunts who'd raised me and hated to disappoint them, I waited for them to approach me on the path.

"We have a request for you," Aunt Enzia said patiently, though she tapped her foot on the ground. Her gauzy wings fluttered behind her before settling. Only a few of our females were born with wings and none had the ability to fly, my aunts among them.

Aunt Rozar nodded pertly. "We do indeed have a request, great-nephew. If you would be so kind as to attend to us for a secunda?"

I bit back my groan. As kind and loving as my aunties were, when they got an idea in their heads, they could be quite demanding and long-winded.

I braced myself for them to speak for some time. How could I do anything else? They'd raised me from the time I was seven-yaros-old, and my parents died in a skimmer accident.

And when she kisses me,

she tastes like a savory roast skarlog.

Skarlog? No, that was not the correct word. One should not refer to the flavor of a dream mate as a side of meat.

Dried morg. That was better. Morg was sweet, and I assumed she would taste sweet as well.

Since it wasn't half-bad, I would write this poem down when I reached my quarters. After I spoke with my aunties, I'd bathed, and we'd eaten in the kitchen, that is.

"What do you need, Aunties?" I asked. Because I hadn't seen them for many dias, I lifted Enzia up to kiss her cheek first, then did the same with Rozar. They were petite, tiny compared to me, and if I didn't pick them up, I had to scrunch my back to reach them.

"We have found her," Enzia said with a fang-baring grin.

"I was going to tell him that," Rozar said with a twist of her lips.

Twins, it was a challenge to tell them apart. Fortunately, they chose not to dress alike. Enzia preferred blue gowns, and Rozar pink, making it easier for the community.

"You have found who?" I asked.

"Someone to teach you the skills you need for the Match-Mating Soiree, of course," Rozar said with a nod.

"I do not wish to attend the soiree," I said with a frown.

I'd ruined things with the last female I tried to mate with, and I would not try again.

"You *do* wish to be mated," Rozar said with affront.

"Not particularly," I grunted.

Enzia gasped. "But how will you have yarlings? We are old." She collapsed against me, but it was all pretend. "If you do not produce soon, we will be too old to help raise them."

"You will live forever," I said, though my hearts twinged. What if they didn't? I loved them; I'd hate to lose them. "As for yarlings, I do wish to hear the patter of their tiny feet in my dwelling."

"Exactly," Enzia said with a sly smile. "This is why we sent your acceptance to attend the soiree."

"You did not," I said sternly, though I could never remain angry with either of them.

"We did," Rozar said pertly. "You have to attend the soiree now. Once there, you will match with someone and bring her home so we can meet her."

I'd gladly plant my seed in a female, but I was too busy on the border to give a female the attention she'd require. And after Shardeene . . .

Enzia looked up at me with limpid eyes. "Please say you will go."

"All right," I grumbled. I could protest, but I'd learned they could always get me to do whatever they pleased, especially if they worked on me together. "I will go to the soiree and tell a female she is to be my mate. We will mate-fast soon after that. I will get her with young, and then I will return to my squadron."

Enzia groaned and tapped my arm. "You cannot do such a thing."

"I thought you wanted yarlings?" I asked, perplexed.

"We do," Rozar said. "But if you hope to mate, you will need to woo her first. One does not just tell a female she will be your mate. Only when she has been wooed will she consent to matefast with you. It would be wrong to matefast with her and leave her for endless patrols. You will need to spend time with her before you will be able to return to the border. Assuming you still wish to do so."

I was missing something here, but I couldn't figure it out. "Why would I not return to the front?"

My aunties looked at each other but said nothing.

It was never good when they were plotting something, but since I could not discern what it might be, I held onto my patience.

Enzia beamed up at me. "Perhaps because you will like your new mate and—"

"You would prefer to spend time with her rather than marching off to the border again," Rozar said, finishing Enzia's sentence, a common thing with them.

"Truly," Enzia said, her tail sweeping back and forth behind her. "We do not understand why these battles are so important to you."

"It is my job."

"Which you do not always need to do. What about your farm?"

Ah, my farm. I'd planted a wellire seed and nurtured it. When it had matured, I hoped to resign my commission in the military and spend the rest of my days digging in the soil. But first, we had to come up with a permanent solution for the Twarvians. I had some ideas I planned to share with my commanding officer during my break.

"Assuredly, sister," Rozar said. She frowned at me. "He has his farm. And once you live there, you could spend your evenings composing music. No more fighting all the time."

"My music sounds atrocious, even to my own ears," I said. I'd tried to absorb their teachings on the peanacharm, but whenever I played, only clangs echoed in the room.

"The delight is in the view of the one standing closest," Rozen said.

"Most definitely, sister." Enzia took her sister's hand and squeezed it. "If you would only practice more, your music would be a wondrous thing to listen to."

I grunted. "Trust me, it will never be wondrous. As for returning to my squadron, you know my job is to keep the Twarvian horde from overrunning our borders."

Enzia tilted her head. "Someone else could do it, could they not?"

"Not at this time," I said with a sigh. "I am needed there."

"You know it distresses us when you are gone," Rozen said. "However, we are currently discussing the Match-Mating Soiree, and before the illustrious event, we have a task for you."

"Several, actually," Enzia said with a snicker. "We have hired someone to teach you how to woo a female."

"You are certain wooing is necessary?" I held up my finger before my aunties could speak. "I suppose I could recite my poetry, and she will swoon and agree to mate with me."

"Please do not recite anything." Enzia rolled her silver eyes that were much like my own. Instead of silver hair like me, however, she and Rozen had inherited fiery copper locks from a distant relative. "I think you should save your poetry until *after* you are matefasted."

"I agree," Rozen said quickly.

My aunties linked their arms through mine and turned me away from the skimmer holding area, leading me to the walkway that wove through town. Our dwelling was located on the end of the main thoroughfare, and we shared the upper level.

"Trust us in this," Rozen said.

"Exactly, sister," Enzia said.

"All right." Would anyone ever enjoy my poetry? "If I do not recite for a mate, how will I win her? I doubt she will wish for me to defeat her in battle, though the prospect has merit." I was only half-joking.

Enzia grumbled. "The person we hired has her work cut out for her, does she not, Rozen?"

"Most definitely."

"Explain," I said, determined to show I was the male of the household and should be listened to in all matters. Well, some of them, that is.

"We filled out an application at the Intergalactic Employment Agency, and they just sent notice," Enzia said.

"A human female is on her way here to teach you the skills you need to woo a mate," Rozen added.

I'd never met a human before. How intriguing.

"What kind of skills are we speaking of?" I was beginning to suspect this "training" would interfere with everything I needed to do in life, namely catching up on my sleep before I needed to return to the border.

"For example, you need to learn how to speak with females," Rozen said.

"Yes, exactly," Enzia said.

We continued along the path weaving through the middle of town we'd planted some distance from the border. Few dared to cultivate wellires close to the wall.

"I speak quite well already," I said, looking up at the milky white wellire on my right. Only two-stories tall, it hadn't fully matured. After one more growing season, it would reach its full height and a colonist family could settle within its upper levels.

Enzia huffed as she shifted aside pale green, lacy vegetation growing too close to the path. I'd come back tomorrow and clip it, before it engulfed the trail. "I agree your language is not always crude, but you—"

"Will not lure a mate by discussing battle," Rozen said, completing the thought. "I suggest you speak of music and flowers."

Music again? "As long as I do not need to *play* music."

"I still say you could if you practiced," Enzia said as we started down the path beside our wellire and continued around to the back of the dwelling.

Durdons dangled from the large, upper part of the plant, their limbs coated with suction cups. They served as the plant's main defense.

One snapped toward Rozen, but I cuffed it, though gently. A latching could leave a painful welt even if it wouldn't kill you.

I'd die to keep the Twarvians from passing the wall, but if some did, they would not find easy entrance to our dwellings.

It was the one thing I could offer my beloved aunties. Well, and my agreement to attend the Match-Mating Soiree.

A broad lawn stretched all the way to the churning river behind our dwelling, and I'd built benches and planted trees, then crafted gardens under my auntie's direction. One would say it was attractive here, though it would not suit for battle. A warrior would trip on one of the many stone creatures my aunties had imported from another planet.

I plucked two buds from a flowerbed and handed one to each of my aunts. Their green faces darkened with joy.

"Flowers are simple," I said. "I will ensure I gift ones to a prospective mate that are open and not ones that have died or wilted."

"Lovely, but there is more to wooing than that," Enzia said, tucking her flower behind her ear. "You need to—"

"Learn how to dance without causing your partner harm, plus how to eat without making a mess," Rozen finished.

"I assume you mean by using eating implements. It would not be polite to heft a hunk of roast and shove it into my mouth." I held in my laugh. Did my aunties believe I was completely unsophisticated?

I wanted to tell them I could handle this myself but pleasing them was important. They would be correct in stating that I bumbled around more than I should. And I did enjoy hefting a hunk of roast and ripping into it with my fangs.

I sighed. "I guess you are right. I do need polishing."

"You need to be domesticated." Rozen tucked the flower into her upswept hair. Its bright yellow color contrasted nicely with her pink gown. "We believe you are perfect just as you are." She hugged me and leaned back in my arms.

Enzia fluttered beside us. She wanted a hug as well. "We want the potential mates to see how wonderful you are. But . . ."

Rozen smiled up at me, her light green face alight with love, flashing the fangs so like my own, only smaller. "But what if something as simple as a polish could make the difference for you? We want you to be happy."

"You believe a mate will do this for me?" What use

would a female have in my life other than bearing my yarlings?

"We want you to find someone to love," Enzia said, edging between me and her sister to claim her hug, which I gladly delivered.

"Love?" I asked. "I do not believe in an emotion like that or want it in my life." After Shardeene, I'd decided love was best for poetry, not reality.

"Of course you do," Rozen said. "You love us, do you not?"

"I do," I said, conceding she was right in that.

"Imagine feeling as if you cannot live without the other person," Enzia said.

"How can I march off to battle if that means leaving someone I care for behind?" I asked.

"Maybe it is time for you to lower your weapons and move to your farm," Rozen said.

I shook my head. "It is not ready for that yet."

Enzia scrunched her face. "Think about it."

"You are correct that I need help if I am to woo a mate," I said.

"We do not tell you this to be mean," Enzia said.

"I know you do not," I said. "I am clumsy. Awkward. And I do not know what to say to someone that does not involve battle strategy or weapons." Which was part of the reason why things had not worked out with Shardeene. That and—

"Not very clumsy," Enzia said, tapping my arm. "You are graceful."

And she was being generous.

This would not be the first time I would be embarrassed at an event. No, I'd fled the last one I attended in disgrace. When I walked onto the dance floor, I tripped over a plant.

It crashed to the floor, spilling soil on the lovely marble tiles. Everyone gaped in my direction. Some pointed and snickered.

And that wasn't all I'd done. While reaching for the ladle to dish up buleene sauce, my big fingers hit my wine glass, spilling ruby liquid across the pristine white table-cloth. And when I stabbed out my knife, aiming to snag a piece of roast layderstork at the same time as my dining partner, I inadvertently ran my knuckles across one of her four breasts. This was better than stabbing her with my knife, correct?

She'd shrieked and hit my arm, and everyone stared—again—in my direction.

I'd left the event after that, deciding there was no way I'd ever impress another female enough to offer them a place by my side. My hearts would slumber, never awoken by another again. I'd never share my glorious poems with a female with ears curling forward to hear each precious word.

"I appreciate you two handling this for me," I said. "It would not have occurred to me to hire someone to teach me these skills. I will work hard to learn from her."

Perhaps this would be all right. When I attended the Match-Mating Soiree, I would not fumble, trip, or insult anyone. I might be able to attract a mate and please my aunts.

As for love, I would avoid the emotion, though it would be nice to like the person I matefasted with.

"When will this teacher arrive?" I asked.

"In a few minue," Enzia said.

I gulped and pawed at my chest. "So soon? I must prepare myself to greet her."

"I am sure she will excuse your warrior sweat, dirt, and

dented armor," Rozen said. She pointed to my face. "And your wound."

Enzia clicked her tongue. "Where did you get that?"

"Battle," I said dryly.

She sighed and shook her head. "You are getting too old for this."

"I am only thirty-two-yaros-old."

"Too old. You are correct, sister," Rozen said.

Enzia grunted. "What can we do but continue to pester him to resign?"

"Nothing, sister, nothing."

"I am right here," I said."

"Of course you are. We are speaking to you, are we not?" Mostly.

"Remember," Enzia shook her finger at me, "this human is here to put a sheen on the great-nephew we love already. She is not here to change you."

"Perhaps I need to be changed."

"No." Enzia cupped my cheeks, making sure my gaze met hers. "Never think for one secunda that you are not special, Forje."

Rozen patted my arm. "You deserve the love you are not sure exists. With a polish, you will find the one who will love you until your dying day."

"Which should not come for a very long time," Enzia said. "If you heed our advice and resign."

"I will consider it." I'd offer nothing else. Until I was confident the Twarvians would no longer attack the colony, I couldn't do anything but help keep them at bay.

A hum erupted overhead, and we watched as a tubelike shuttle soared across the sky to land behind our dwelling. With a big hiss, the vehicle settled, and the lid lifted.

When a bare leg projected from the open hatch, my aunties gasped.

We watched as the leg latched onto the side of the craft. A lush, rounded buttock encased in black fabric followed. The person grappled with the edge of the shuttle before tumbling over the side.

As I rushed forward, she collapsed on the ground.

CHAPTER THREE
KALEI

"Is she dead?" a female cried from somewhere nearby.

"That would be tragic," a different female whimpered. "She just got here. We need her."

"Exactly, sister," the first said.

I lay with my face buried in pale blue grass. My head pounded, and my mouth tasted as if a flock of birds had nested there recently. I suspected they'd pooped while they hung out too.

A male grunted. "She is not dead."

"Then why is she lying there?" one of the females asked.

"A very good question, sister."

"Do you believe she is tired?"

"I know," the second shouted. "She has swooned! How romantic."

"Why is swooning romantic?" the male asked. "If I did that, I would be engulfed by a Twarvian."

One of the women grunted. "You know very well that the Twarvians do not come here."

"Because I keep them away," he said. "This is why I believe I must—"

"Forje, please," one of the women said. "The fact that you do nothing about this situation shows us why you need domestication. The human female has swooned. You were supposed to catch her, sweep her off her feet—"

"And kiss her," the second female said, finishing the sentence for the first seamlessly, like they were two individual beings attached at the hip. Perhaps they were.

"No kissing," I bellowed, lifting my head that continued to spin.

Welcome to stasis lag. I hadn't yet had the luxury of traveling this way, but I'd read about the dangers of the drugs used to keep a traveler suspended until they arrived at their destination.

Some women got horny from stasis, while other vomited.

It appeared I was unable to make my limbs cooperate with whatever I asked them to do.

"Ugh," I said, prying myself up off the ground. I leaned against one of the shuttle legs, taking in two female and one male alien, all watching me with wide eyes. Far away in the sky, a planet orbited this one with rings resembling Saturn.

Even more bizarre, a giant, milky white mushroom had sprouted like a three-story building behind them. I had to be dreaming.

"You must sweep her off her feet," the pale green alien female wearing a blue gown said, waving to the alien male.

"Yes, do," the other female, this one wearing pink, said. She flicked her hand toward me. "We will watch and give comment."

"This is so delightful, sister," the first said, baring very pointy fangs.

The big, light green, armor-covered warrior with a

network of scars on his face, exposed arms, and chest stomped over and stopped in front of me. He stared down with what looked like hope—but it had to be dismay—in his gorgeous silver eyes. Hair in a lighter silver flowed around his shoulders, and I wondered if it was as silky as it appeared. Horns jutted from his thick tresses, curving up over the top of his head before coming to blunted tips on the back of his crown.

Brawny, he looked like he'd stepped off the stage of an alien weightlifting competition, donned some armor, and was currently posing for the audience.

"Ugh?" he asked.

"Yes, ugh." I clutched my head. "I imagine I should introduce myself, but I'm finding it a challenge to stand, let alone talk."

"You have swooned," he said. "I am supposed to sweep you up." Without waiting for me to do more than sputter, he stooped down and lifted me off my feet with his arms around my waist, holding me with my belly facing down and my head dangling close to the ground.

"Oh, not like that, nephew," the blue gowned lady said. "Flip her over and cradle her like a yarling."

The pink dressed alien shook her head in dismay. "See, sister? This is why I said he needed training. He will never get close to claiming a mate if he treats her like this."

"I am the one who said that; you may very well remember, Rozen."

"It was me, Enzia," Rozen said. "I said it."

"No, me," Enzia said firmly.

"Aunties," the guy grumbled. "Show me how to do this?"

"Flip her over," Rozen said.

Enzia rushed toward us. "Carefully! She is not a Twar-vian in need of stabbing."

Stabbing?

"I know this, Aunties," he said with a sigh.

"Put me down," I said.

He tossed me up into the air, high enough I soared above all three of them. When I tumbled back down, shrieking, he caught me, holding me like a bride being carried across a threshold.

"Is this the swoon position?" he asked the pale green ladies.

They nodded, flashing pointy fangs my way.

One caught my eye. "I am Enzia, and my lovely sister here is Rozen. You, my dear, are being held by our great-nephew, Forje."

"He doesn't need to hold me," I said, though I wasn't sure I could remain on my feet without support yet. Between stasis and my recent gymnastic feat, courtesy of Forje, my brain wouldn't stop spinning.

"We must get her inside," Enzia said, starting toward the big mushroom.

"I knew we should have imported that fainting couch," Rozen said, catching up to Enzia. Sweeping ahead of us, they aimed for the giant mushroom that I now noted had a pale blue cap with darker blue spots. They left the big, cute alien guy standing by the shuttle holding me.

"My bag," I cried as he walked after them. It wasn't much, but it would be nice to change out of my mourning clothing.

"Of course." He pivoted and brought me back to the craft, leaning forward so I could snatch the handle from the upper compartment.

As he strode toward the back of the giant mushroom, the shuttle took off, soaring toward the sky.

"I'm Kalei," I said. "Kalei Bridget Sutherland." Because it felt odd keeping my hands clenched on my chest, I put them around his neck. He had delightful muscles along his shoulders, outlined by the leather straps of his armor. He was warm, too, and cozy, despite his rippling bulk.

"I am Forje Kox Traach'eol. You may call me Forje."

"Cocks?" I gulped.

He paused on the grassy path, scrunching his unusual eyebrow at me. Thin spikes jutted off the surface like straight eyebrow lashes. Were they soft? I'd discovered his hair was.

"Is she swooning again?" Enzia called out from an opening at the base of the mushroom.

They lived here?

"They are conversing sister," Rozen said. "See? My idea of hiring someone to teach him social graces is paying off. She must be correcting his diction and pronunciation already. Do grab her bag. We can place it in her room."

"Yes, yes, I will. This is wonderful sister but do remember that *I* am the one who thought of this brilliant idea." Enzia swept inside the thick mushroom stem with her sister following.

"Do not linger on the lawn, Forje," one of them called from inside. "She might swoon once again, and she should do so inside."

"Do we have anything for lightheadedness, sister?"

"We should look in the kitchen."

Their voices faded while I wondered what I'd gotten myself into.

The skin on Forje's forehead crinkled again, wiggling

the spikes projecting from his unibrow. "*Kox* is my middle name, not *cocks*."

"I'm sorry." Did ditz brain come with stasis?

"It is not a problem." He took wooden steps up onto a broad platform spanning the back of the mushroom, his black boots thudding on the wooden surface.

"Are you my boss?" I asked.

"One could say this. My aunties placed the advertisement, but I am the person you will be teaching." He flashed his fangs, something I'd found vaguely creepy when his aunts did it. On him, it was decidedly sexy.

Since he was my boss, I shouldn't be thinking he was sexy. I'd shut that part of my brain off.

Sure.

Actually, I was here to train him so he could woo a mate, who would not be me. It would be best if I remembered that. Besides, after Rich nearly forced me into an untenable situation, it would be nice to extend my no-matchmating hiatus.

"I can walk," I said.

"Oh, yes, I am sure you can." He crossed the open deck. Big planters overflowing with flowers stood on either side of the back door. He kicked the door, and the panel swung inward.

"In here, in here," one of the female aliens called from ahead.

Forje strode into a stem tunnel and quickly climbed a long flight of stairs leading to the blue polka dot cap above. Exiting, he strode through a big kitchen with opaque "windows" along one wall and strangely enough, normal-appearing cooking implements sitting on the counter. I spied a synthesizer and other devices I'd never seen before.

The floor looked soft and squishy, but there wasn't time

to examine it. Forje left the kitchen and strode down a narrow hallway beyond.

At the end of the hall—with squishy, membranous doors on either side—he entered a small open area with stairs shooting up the left side.

A crook of my head showed at least one level above us —all within the cap. This was amazing.

Enzia stood in an open doorway on the right. "We have prepared the sofa for her." She flashed me another nail-biting smile. "We apologize for not purchasing a swooning couch in advance of your arrival. Our sofa should substitute nicely, however." She backed into the room as Forje crossed the foyer.

I took in the profusion of weapons mounted on the walls. I had to be dreaming. We weren't inside a living mushroom, were we?

"Interesting decorations," I said, grateful my head had stopped spinning. Funny how I focused on that, and not the giant mushroom.

"I have battled with each one," he said.

"Outside, you mentioned you thought I could walk, so why are you still carrying me?" I asked.

"I do apologize." He came to a stop and lowered me to my feet. "My aunties told me this was the appropriate way to carry a female."

My brain decided this was a great time to flip completely over, but thankfully, I didn't fall—*swoon*, that is.

"Are you all right?" he asked, scowling.

"Yes." I stared down at the floor that felt like a big pillow beneath my feet. "Your home is alive?"

"Of course it is. We brought wellire seeds with us when we came to this planet and planted them. Our wellires grew over the next three seasons, and now we all have homes."

This was incredible.

"In here," one of the ladies said, "Forje. Lay her in here."

"I must lay you in the parlor," he said, lifting me up and tossing me over his shoulder.

While I sputtered, he strode into another room with more opaque windows along the outer wall. They curved along the cap of the mushroom. The inside of the dwelling was pale pink, but the furniture appeared like what I'd find back on Earth.

"Forje," Enzia chided. "Must you carry her that way? All the blood is rushing to her head. It will pool there, and she will have—"

"A headache," Rozen said.

He flipped me down over his chest and laid me on a ginormous sofa that would be the perfect size for his enormous body. I wasn't a huge person, so it reminded me of the fairytale where a blonde girl sat in a big bear's chair before trying another, finding neither of them were just right.

"Once you are no longer swooning," Forje told me, "I will take you to your rooms, and you will rest."

The two ladies beamed, their wrinkly faces creasing with their smiles.

"I just slept for . . . I don't know how long," I said. "What planet is this?"

"Davoome, in the Wreslar Quadrant. Our home is called the Haehron colony because we are all Haehron."

Even before entering the Intergalactic Employment Agency, I'd vaguely heard about the Haehron. I recalled something about them having to abandon their planet for this one. Another species had been relocated here also, but the two didn't get along.

I sat up against the arm of the sofa and stretched my

legs out in front of me, my feet unable to reach the low table between the sofa and a couple chairs.

The three of them stood nearby, watching me.

"Drink this," Rozen said, leaning forward to thrust a glass into my hands.

I stared down at the pale pink liquid. "What is it?"

"A soothing balm. It will prevent you from swooning again."

The "swooning" came from stasis, which should wear off soon. And the fact that I was inside a giant mushroom. I took in the squares between the windows made up of slats, perhaps to let in air.

Staring at the drink, I reminded myself I was going to live here with them. They'd hired me. Surely, they wouldn't try to poison me the moment I arrived. With that thought in mind, I took a sip, finding it watery, sweet, and floral, but pleasant enough to drain the glass.

I handed it back. "Thank you."

They watched me eagerly, and I started to wonder what was in that drink. But when I didn't get nausea or anything, I scooted forward on the sofa to dangle my feet over the side, though I comically couldn't reach the floor. "Would you like to get started right away?"

Since I had to crook my neck to look at Forje, I jumped to the floor, holding onto the sofa. At five-seven, I was used to being around taller people, but he towered over me by at least a foot and a half.

It made me feel tiny and precious, something I shouldn't be feeling.

"Working already? What a delightful idea," Enzia said, clapping her hands.

"I agree, sister," Rozen said. She stared at me eagerly.

"How do you propose to teach our great-nephew sophistication?"

"It will take time," I said. "When's the Match-Mating Soiree?"

"In two dias," he said.

"Oh." That wasn't much time. However, he spoke in an articulate manner, and other than dangling me in various positions and his current state of undress, he shouldn't be too hard to whip into shape. He might not need much training.

"How do you propose to handle this?" he asked.

I lifted my wrist, displaying my com. "Why don't we start by making a list of the activities that will take place at the Match-Mating Soiree? Then we can pick away at each until you feel confident you can handle anything that might pop up during that event."

"You will not swoon during our discussion?" he asked, his brow spikes wiggling again.

"I'll do my best not to." My stasis lag was wearing off, and I didn't feel like I was going to collapse on the squishy mushroom floor. "The sooner we get started, the quicker you'll be ready, right?"

"Yes, very much so," Rozen said.

Enzia leaned against her sister. "She is a delight, is she not? We selected well."

Actually, the Intergalactic Employment Agency had selected me, but if these three were happy, so was I.

"We can start with clothing," I said. "I'm sure you don't plan to attend dressed like that."

He peered down at his chest. "What is wrong with how I am dressed?"

"You can't wear weapons to a soiree where you hope to meet a future mate."

"Why not?"

"Because others might feel threatened."

Enzia and Rozen watched us raptly, their heads snapping back in forth in unison. Did they plan to watch us the entire time I worked with Forje?

"I will wear my weapons to the soiree," he declared. "That is *not* negotiable."

"Why would you need them at a function like that? It's formal, correct?"

"I will need them to defend myself."

"From what?"

"Threats," he said grimly.

CHAPTER FOUR
FORJE

"Will there be wild beasts at the soiree?" Kalei gulped, her pretty brown eyes widening. I'd never seen brown eyes before. Almost everyone I knew had silver. They were warm, soft. I wanted to stroke them. Not her eyeballs, per se, but the black spikes jutting around them.

"There are threats everywhere," I said grimly. Surely, she didn't expect a warlord to go anywhere without his weapons. What if something attacked?

"I agree with Kalei," Enzia said. "You should not bring weapons to the soiree."

Rozen turned to Enzia. "I believe this is why he suffered a mishap the last time we attended an event, is that not correct, sister?"

"It must have been horrifying to trip on a sword," Enzia said.

I shot them a glare. "I did not trip on my sword."

Rozen turned to Enzia. "He did."

"You are correct, sister." Enzia gave us a pert nod. "He did."

"What happened?" Kalei asked.

I groaned, not wishing to explain this to her. "It is best to forget."

Enzia trotted over to Kalei and lowered her voice. "Our great-nephew does his best. He is the sweetest yarling."

"I am a fully grown male," I growled, feeling as if this conversation was galloping away without me. I bowed to my aunties. "Leave."

"What?" Enzia asked, her spine stiffening.

Rozen snickered. "Perhaps he only wishes for *me* to be present during his first lesson."

"You need to leave as well," I told Aunt Rozen.

"What?" she echoed Enzia. "Do you not wish us to remain here to give Kalei pointers?"

Kalei's pretty eyes widened.

"No," I snapped, though I wasn't irritated with them. How could I think, let alone do as Kalei might suggest, with my aunties chattering like mayflits? "Actually, would you both be so kind as to prepare an evening meal for us? I am hungry." I met Kalei's gaze. "Are you hungry? If they prepare a meal, you could teach me a bit about eating with the proper implements."

"What a wonderful idea," Enzia gushed.

Rozen scurried toward the foyer. "I agree."

Enzia hurried after her, her gossamer wings fluttering. "I know just what we can prepare. A roast skarlog would be very tasty."

"If we add a souvlette, it will require multiple eating implements," Rozen crowed. "I believe a brulaveete and a compest as well."

Enzia grinned as she left the room. "Such delightful ideas, sister."

My breath whooshed out as they left the room, and I

followed to engage the panel behind them. I leaned my back against it and watched Kalei, taking in her rich, dark hair and petite form. She was lovely, something I had not expected to notice. She was my teacher, not a potential mate.

And why had that thought occurred to me?

Her skin gleamed in the late-day sunshine . . .

her lush form ripe and succulent.

It would be easy to craft poems about Kalei.

Succulent wasn't quite the right word, but for some reason, I didn't wish to sit and explore other options. I wanted to stand near Kalei and listen to whatever she had to say.

"I *am* hungry," she said with a soft smile. "Thanks for thinking of that." She gestured to one of the chairs, as she hopped back up onto the sofa. "Have a seat, and we can go through the soiree and see where you feel you need the most help. Perhaps outlining that and dining will be enough for today?"

I dropped into the chair opposite her while she accessed her com.

"Where will the soiree take place?" she asked.

"On the Plushier Space Station."

She entered the information into her com. "How long will it take to get there from here?"

"A few horuses."

"That's good." She leaned back against the cushions. "Two dias to get you ready isn't much time. You know that, correct?"

"Yes. Can you make me . . .?"

"What?" She watched me with such intensity, it almost cut into my skin. Heat flared inside me, and for a minue, I was disconcerted, because I didn't know what this meant. I wasn't sure I liked feeling this way. Only once before, I'd gotten excited about a female only to ruin it when we took things too far too soon. If only I'd waited until after I'd told her everything.

I swallowed. "Can you make me less clumsy and more appealing to females?" Then I wouldn't offend the next one.

Sadness filled her eyes. "Has it occurred to you that someone should love you the way you are?"

A notion I was better not thinking about. "No."

Her head tilted. "Why not? I'm not trying to put myself out of a job, but I'm sure you're special just as you are. I'll be happy to help you change the parts of yourself you don't like, and everyone can benefit from a polish, but keep that in mind. You're going to the Match-Mating Soiree to find a mate you'll spend the rest of your life with, unless divorce is common among your species."

"It is not." Another odd notion. My translator told me what divorce meant, but I hadn't heard of anyone ending a relationship with their mate before. Fated ones were meant to be together for always.

Perhaps if Shardeene had been my—

"My point is you want to find someone you're compatible with. Even better if you can find someone to love."

"Love is an odd notion," I said, feeling as if I floundered deep within my mind. A cavern had opened that was never there before. "Mating is often done to secure a truce or combine families to enhance wealth."

"Marriages—matings—sometimes take place on Earth for the same reasons, but I just wanted to put it out there. Life is too short to spend it with someone you don't love."

"I am not sure I believe in love." Despite sitting still on the chair, my body and my mind felt as if they'd been thrown into a storm-ridden sea with no shore in sight. I could swim, but where would I go?

Her face softened. "I'm not sure I do either."

"Why don't you believe in love?"

She shrugged. "I've loved people, but I don't believe that's what we're discussing here. My great-aunt raised me—"

"My great-aunties raised me."

"Something we have in common. Your aunts are sweet. My aunt was amazing too. My parents died when I was little, and she insisted I come live with her. When I got older, and she was sick, I took care of her, a small price to pay for all she'd done for me. She died eight yaros ago, and I ended up caring for my ex-husband's mother who had cancer. She recently died as well."

"And this is why you do not believe in love? Because they die?" I'd noted she mentioned an ex-mate, and I wanted to quiz her about that.

A frown filled her face. "That's an interesting thought, but . . ." Her head tilted. "I loved them. As for the love one might have for a mate, that didn't work out. He . . . It's best not to talk about him, I suppose. Maybe there's someone new out there for me, or maybe there isn't. Sometimes, it seems unbelievable that I could care for someone so much that I'd do anything to make them happy. My aunt and Duchess Viola did that." She sniffed and wiped her eyes, showing me the depth of the love she'd felt for those who'd died. It was admirable, and it showed me she would do all she could to help me. "What about you? Why don't *you* believe in love?"

"Like you, I love my aunties. They are special. But . . ."

"But what?"

"When I think of attending the soiree and picking a

female from those offered for mating, I don't want emotions combining with this choosing."

"Maybe you'll meet someone and fall fast."

Was that possible?

When I looked at Kalei, my emotions churned through me like I was the mythical dessolire soaring through vast caverns, free and unfettered. Some wished to trap the creature, though no one had. It was said if you did, they'd grant one wish to regain their precious freedom.

What if . . . It was silly and not even a bit rational but . . .

What if I was granted such a wish, and I asked for Kalei?

CHAPTER FIVE

KALEI

We didn't talk more about feelings, which was good as far as I was concerned. The last thing I wanted to discuss was my failed marriage with Rich.

We continued going through what he might expect at the upcoming event, and the task ahead of me appeared daunting unless he was savvier with dining, dancing, and social interaction than he let on.

By the time we'd laid out a plan for the next two dias, our meal was ready.

"We can work on dining habits and ways to engage your partner while we eat," I said as we strode down the hall, following Enzia and Rozen chatting quietly ahead of us. I peered around, still surprised they lived inside a big mushroom. "Did you carve this?"

"I cultivated the wellire as it was growing, directing how it formed its insides."

"That's amazing."

He grinned, and my heart flipped when it shouldn't. "Thank you." He patted the wall, and I swore the mushroom released a soft sigh. "It lives for us and us for it."

"What do you mean?"

"My aunties would call the topic indelicate."

Pausing, I frowned. "Tell me."

"Along with the moisture it sucks from the ground that contains nutrients, it stays alive by consuming our waste. In exchange, it allows us to live inside its dotted cap."

Waste? Oh, yuck. But I guessed everything needed to eat, and it was a good use for something we'd otherwise have to bury. It was best not to think about the living walls made out of . . . poop. Well, digested poop, that is.

"See?" he said with a chuckle. "I told you my aunties would consider it indelicate."

"They're right."

"Inside here," Enzia called out as she entered a room on the left side of the pseudo-hall.

At the doorway, Forje and I tried to enter at the same time. His sword rubbed across my leg, and I winced.

"I, um . . ." he said, bowing.

"Truly, great-nephew, you should start there," Rozen said. "Always gesture for the female to enter the room ahead of you. That would be the polite thing to do."

"Back in the hall," he barked at me.

I lifted one eyebrow. "Do you always talk to females like this?"

His brow furrowed before clearing. "Ah. You suggest it is impolite for me to tell you what to do."

"If you take nothing else from my teachings, you'll win points with that alone."

"Would you be so kind as to return to the hallway with me?" he asked. He was laying it on a bit thick, but everyone started somewhere.

"Thank you," I said.

Outside the dining area, he gestured grandly for me to

enter first. His sword swept out at his side when he bowed, making me scoot back away from him.

"Perhaps you can take . . . shorter weapons to the soiree if you still insist on wearing them?" I asked. "I'm sure no one would find a knife or two upsetting."

"What a brilliant idea," he said.

"I imagine we'll find compromise is the best way to handle all this. I want you to feel as if you can be yourself while showing your best side to your potential matches."

He flashed me a shy smile. "I like this."

As I entered the room ahead of him, I tried not to think about the butlierflees dancing in my belly from his smile. He was not only attractive; his shy ways made him very appealing. Truly, if he showed himself in this light, females would climb all over him.

I glided into the dining room with him right behind.

Enzia and Rozen stood near an open door on the right side of the room, beaming our way.

I took in the table with chairs enough for six diners. They'd set the table for two. In addition to the furniture, the plates, etc., looked like something I'd find back on Earth. I assumed they purchased them from an interstellar department store and shipped them here.

"We thought we would serve you to give you the chance to work with Forje," Enzia said. "There will be five courses tonight."

How had they whipped that up so fast?

"An excellent idea," I said, walking over to stand beside one of the chairs.

Forje trooped around the table to the other side, his weapons clanking, and hauled his chair out to sit.

Rozen cleared her throat.

He frowned in her direction, then looked at me, still

standing. He blinked for a minue. "I should do something before sitting."

"It's considered polite to hold a lady's chair while she sits, then assist her in pushing it closer to the table."

Enzia nodded. "It is the same here."

A relief. I'd hate to teach him things that could be misinterpreted.

"Do ladies have problems with their arms?" he asked, frowning. "Perhaps you should train with me to strengthen them."

"It is a polite thing to do, nephew," Rozen said.

"Ah. Polite." He seemed to taste the world. "Then I shall do it." He stomped around to my side of the table and pulled out my chair. Once I was seated, he lifted the entire chair with me on it and tucked it beneath the table.

"Thank you," I said. "You don't need to lift the chair, however. A gentle nudge is all we need."

He continued to blink down at me. "If you are weak and cannot bring your chair closer by yourself, why not lift it and place you where you wish it to be?"

"We're quite capable of moving our chair by ourselves. But like opening a door for someone to be kind when we can do that as well is a sign of respect."

"I . . . all right." He pivoted and returned to his side of the table, crinkling me a smile. "Who will urge my chair forward?"

My laugh spurted out. "If I did it for you, you'd have to get up and do it again for me. We'd be here all night helping each other bring our chairs into the right position."

"You are correct. Besides," he placed both fists against his chest, "I am a mighty warrior and capable of moving both your chair and mine."

I shook my head at his antics.

"We will serve now?" Enzia asked.

"Yes, thank you," I said.

"As I said, we have prepared five courses," Rozen called over her shoulder as the two sisters scooted through the door and into the kitchen.

They returned quickly and each placed a small dish in front of us. Whatever it was, it had been beautifully presented.

"This is lovely," I said, studying the pale pink circular foamy-appearing appetizer with tiny orange curls placed artfully on top. A light, darker pink sauce swirled across the plate and the dish. I glanced toward Forje. "Which would be a nice thing to say to your dining partner."

"It is lovely, is it not?" he said carefully.

"Great job." It was always good to give praise. "For the first course, we use our—"

He lifted the item with his fingers and popped it into his mouth. His eyes closed, and he shifted on his seat, groaning as he chewed.

My breath stuttered out. I should be correcting him, but all I could think of was him lying on a bed completely naked while I licked his body. He'd move like this. Groan like this.

Heat shot through me.

For the first time, I realized my new boss was hot.

And now that I'd opened pandora's box and he leapt out of it, there would be no stuffing him back inside.

CHAPTER SIX

FORJE

"So," Kalei said. "We don't usually eat our food with our hands."

"Why not?" I asked, swallowing the last of the tiny item. It tasted good, and I wondered why they'd only brought one for each of us and not a full platter of them.

"We usually eat simply," Aunt Rozen hastened to say to Kalei. "One course. But we thought it would be best to serve many this evening so that you could teach Forje what implement to use with each."

"I will," she said, smiling my way. Something had changed in her eyes. Was she upset that I hadn't waited to learn which device to use with the tiny bite?

If I didn't know better, I'd think the look in her eyes— and the way her tiny tongue dipped out to lick her upper lip —meant she was attracted to me.

I'd never met a human before, which meant I had to be misreading her expression. She was not attracted to a scarred brute like me.

"I am sorry," I said. "I should have waited for instruction, correct?"

She shrugged, and a smile lit her face. "The appetizer must be good because you were groaning over there as if . . ." Her eyes widened. "Well . . . as if you were enjoying it."

"I did." I was puzzled. Why would my groaning about the taste of something lead to her attraction?

One minue. I wasn't stupid. I'd been with females before, though not in over a yaro since Shardeene and I—

My lovely human teacher found me sexually appealing? How intriguing.

Her lips were pinker than the underbelly of a destideen . . .

No, that didn't sound right. Not a destideen but a . . . a foogar. Yes, the underbelly of a foogar.

"What's that about my lips?" she asked, studying my face.

Had I spoken aloud? A glance at my aunties, whose bodies twitched as they held in laughter, suggested I *had* spoken the line from my new poem.

"I did not refer to your lips," I said, lying outright.

"Okay." The word came out with her low laugh that socked me in the gut like a destideen, stealing my breath. It took me a minue to catch it. "Getting back to the first course." She looked down quickly before glancing back up, her gaze meeting mine in an almost shy manner. "Let me split mine with you." She stretched her arm across the table. "Give me your plate."

"Oh, we have more," Enzia said. "Allow me to retrieve another from the kitchen."

It was awkward learning social table graces while my aunties watched, but I got the feeling if I asked them to remain in the kitchen, I'd hurt their feelings. They'd brought Kalei here, and they were excited to watch her turn me from a bumbling warrior into a suave, sophisticated Haehron noble worthy of attracting a mate.

I'd promised, so I would try harder to listen before acting.

Enzia returned with a second portion of the tasty treat, but I decided not to mention that I was grateful she'd brought a couple of them. One bite would not fill me after I'd spent the day in combat.

She lowered the plate in front of me, and I kept my hands at my sides, watching Kalei.

"Generally, if you're not sure what eating implement to use, start from the outside." She lifted the dining spire farthest to the left of her plate, and I did the same, fumbling with it. It sprung from my fingers, clattering on the table.

I looked up, expecting to see scorn, but only smooth patience filled her face.

"I apologize," I said.

"No worries. Watch."

With a delicate touch, she minced off a tiny bit of the pink appetizer, slid the tongs beneath it and lifted it to her mouth, carefully placing the bite on her luscious tongue.

Luscious tongue? I frowned. Why was I thinking about Kalei's tongue as anything other than something she used to eat?

As she chewed and swallowed, even doing that in a delicate manner, my cock twitched.

My body had no business getting involved with this. Kalei was eating. There was nothing sexy about that.

Yet Kalei eating *was* sexy.

"This is delicious," she told my Aunties, who beamed. Kalei's attention returned to me. "Now you try."

Frankly, I wanted to do something about my cock that kept jerking upward against my pants. In a minue, it would nudge the underside of the table, and I had a feeling lifting the table with it would not be considered an act of sophistication.

I was a gritty warrior, nothing else.

A gritty warrior who needed to smooth his edges.

Dining spire. I needed to keep my focus on the task and not my cock or what I'd like to do with it.

Taking a cue from her, I delicately lifted the dining spire and sliced through what was barely a taste of the tidbit. I carefully nudged the prongs beneath the sliver and lifted it, forcing a smile Kalei's way. I placed the slice in my mouth and despite the wonderful flavors, all of this felt . . . shallow.

That was the right word. *Shallow.* And I'd found the word without working on a poem.

"Very good," Kalei said, watching me. Shadows slid through her eyes. Did she see that pretending to be someone other than who I truly was made me sad?

"Tell you what," she said, tossing her dining spire onto the table. She lifted what was left of her appetizer with her fingers and popped it into her mouth, wiggling on her seat with her eyes closed while she savored the delicacy. "Mmmm. Thish ish amazing."

When her eyes opened, they sparkled.

She *did* see.

Knowing we could communicate in this subtle way made something shift inside me, as if a bit of me slid away, exposing a vulnerable part of my soul I hadn't known existed.

I'd already decided she was attracted to me.

The most interesting thing about this situation was that *I* was also attracted to *her*.

CHAPTER SEVEN

KALEI

We worked through the five courses. Each time, I told him which implement worked best for the dish, with an explanation. I wanted him to know which was correct even if he chose not to use it. He appeared to be a quick study.

We also talked about polite conversation, and by the frown brewing on his forehead, this warrior found discussing the weather and clothing choices boring. So did I for that matter.

During other times, when I could tell I was losing him to either frustration or dismay, I lifted the delectable treat and munched on it while groaning about the wonderful flavors. Truly, Enzia and Rozen could work at the best restaurants and command the highest chef prices.

"I'll be at the soiree, but I assume I'll wait in my room and give instruction to you outside the event," I said.

"You are coming with me to each activity, are you not?" He glanced at Enzia and Rozen, who nodded vigorously.

"A wonderful idea," Rozen said.

"Oh, I—"

"Exactly, sister," Enzia said. "We would not dream of anything else." Her gaze fell on me. "I believe it would be best for you to remain near our great-nephew throughout the soiree to guide him as needed."

"How long is the soiree?" Frankly, I was a bit dismayed to learn I'd come all this way to only work two days. The Agency hadn't made that part of the assignment clear.

"The soiree lasts for three dias," Enzia said.

So, five altogether. It still wasn't long.

"We'll be on the space station the entire time?" I asked.

"Yes." She glanced at her sister. "We must arrange for quarters for Kalei as well."

"Most definitely," Rozen said.

Forje watched me. Did I read hope in his eyes? Probably. He wanted to find a mate, and a guy like him deserved the best. I could already tell that while he was brawny and hardened on the outside, he was sweet and squishy on the inside. If someone hurt him, well, I'd smack her.

"I'll be happy to go with you," I said with a smile. "Then I can give you subtle guidance from the sidelines."

"Thank you," he said softly.

My job would finish at the end of the soiree, however. Where would I go from there? I wasn't confident the Interstellar Employment Agency had an office in this small colony, though they must have a branch on the space station. I'd look into it when I was on board.

I had nothing waiting for me back on Earth other than a few friends I'd reach out to once I landed someplace new. And Rich, who might still pursue me. Would he really take things that far?

He had when his mother wasn't around to smack the back of his hand.

It might be wise to find work on the space station. Surely someone would need my skills.

When we finished, I sat back and yawned. I might've overcome the stasis lag, but I hadn't had real sleep in a very long time.

"You are tired," Forje said. "You must be exhausted."

For a warlord who spent much of his time battling creatures, he was surprisingly savvy about the situation. And kind, like his aunts. I liked it here already, and I'll be sad when I leave.

I was here to domesticate him so he could lure in a mate, when all I wanted to do was . . .

Okay, I wanted to lure him close to me instead.

The thought was totally inappropriate. I was an employee. He was essentially my boss, though Enzia and Rozen had officially hired me. But I couldn't . . . I wasn't sure what was happening. My emotions churned around inside me. Maybe my trepidation came from my abrupt departure from Earth. I wasn't sure about the true cause.

I wasn't starting to fall for this big, brutishly handsome alien guy, was I?

Nah. It wasn't possible. I'd just met him.

"Allow me to show you to your quarters," he said, rising from the table.

"A splendid idea, nephew," Enzia said. She took Rozen's arm and dragged her toward the kitchen. "We will wash the dishes and arrange for quarters for Kalei on the space station."

"I could stay with you two if it's a problem," I said.

"Oh, we are not going to the soiree," Enzia said.

"Why not?"

"Because we have duties here, don't we, Rozen?"

"We surely do."

They scooted into the kitchen, the door closing behind them.

Forje came around the table.

"If you're in a situation like this at the soiree," I said. "And you're about to leave the dining room and move to another room for, perhaps, dancing, you could offer a female your arm."

"I need my arms," he said, though his twinkling eyes told me he was joking. He chuckled. "My aunts believe I am rough and unpolished, but in some ways, they are wrong."

"Perhaps they don't see you for who you truly are?"

He eased my chair back and straightening, held out his arm. "Perhaps they do not."

I sensed there was more to Forje than the person he projected on the surface.

"Allow me to escort you to your room," he said, guiding me toward the door to the hall. In the foyer, he urged me up the stairs.

"It looks like you have two stories within the cap," I said. "The top must be smaller than the lower level because the outer layer of the wellire curves upward. Do all of you have rooms on the second floor?"

"We do. There is an office, as well, where I conduct affairs on a dash."

"You're in the military?" I asked as we reached the second story. Like the first level, the walls were pale pink and the floor felt like a firm pillow beneath my feet. He said he'd cultivated the wellire, urging it into this shape, which I found unbelievable. If I wasn't seeing it with my own eyes, I wouldn't believe this was real.

"I have served in our military for many yaros," he said.

"How old are you?"

"Thirty-two-yaros-old."

"I'm twenty-eight."

We started down an open area on the right with a molded half-wall on the inside to keep us from falling to the level below. This level was mirrored on the left, and I noted three doors on each side, presumably leading to bedrooms and his office.

"Enzia and Rozen have rooms over there." He waved to the opposite level. "Spare rooms are located on this side, including the one you will use while you are here."

"Thank you," I said softly. I wanted to ask where his room was, but I didn't want to come across as too forward.

He paused outside the panel farthest down on the left. "You thank me for offering you a place to sleep at night?" His grin told me he was teasing. "How could we do anything less?"

"I left Earth in a hurry. As I said, my former boss died."

His humor faded. "I am sorry. Were you close?"

"She was a friend, but she was also my ex-husband's mother. I cared for the Duchess, as everyone called her, for two yaros. She was strict but sweet, and I miss her."

"Why leave in a hurry, then?"

How much should I tell him? I shrugged. It wasn't like Rich would follow me here. "My ex-husband offered me a new position, but it was in his bed."

A growl ripped up Forje's throat, and his hand went to the largest weapon sheathed on his belt. "Would you like me to go to Earth and kill him?"

"It's nice of you to offer, but why endanger your freedom for something like that?"

"He insulted you. Killing him would not endanger my freedom."

"On Earth, the authorities don't like it when you kill

someone. They'd arrest you, put you to trial, and if you lost your case, they'd imprison you."

Another growl rumbled in his chest. "Here, insulting a female in such a way could be punishable by death."

How refreshing. "On Earth, sadly, it's common for males to insult females."

"How sad for you all." He shook his head, his long silver hair sliding across his shoulders. It was thick and silky, and I wondered what it would be like to bury my face in the strands.

"You're right." I couldn't imagine walking down a street or going to a store without a guy calling out to me, offering me something sleezy. Did any guy believe that worked as a pick-up line? They must, or they wouldn't do it.

Or they were desperate. Or irritated. Both.

"Allow me to show you where everything is inside your room," he said, swinging open the door. "I will bring your bag up in a few minue."

That's right. I left it in the foyer.

We stepped into a big room with three windows mounted on the outer wall. While we were eating, the sun had set. The Saturn-like planet had fled the sky, but three moons had risen, each equally round and shedding pale pink light.

"Pretty," I said, crossing the room to look out a window.

"I agree."

I turned to find him standing beside me, but he was watching me, not the moons.

He swallowed hard, his gaze focusing on my mouth. For one second, I thought he was going to kiss me, something that would both surprise and please me. I shouldn't have wanted to kiss him, but I did. I couldn't stop thinking about what his mouth would feel like pressed against mine.

"Through the door on the right, you will find a cleansing unit," he said, suddenly backing away from me. "There is also a fabricator, plus an evacuation unit, though that feeds directly into our wellire."

That was going to take some getting used to.

"Will it be all right for me to make some clothing? I didn't bring anything appropriate for a soiree." I didn't *own* anything appropriate for a soiree, but I didn't need to share that much. The Duchess had paid a decent wage, and the position came with room and board, but after personal necessities and clothing, there wasn't a lot left. I'd saved all I could, but my balance would drop quickly if I had to use credits to fabricate ballgowns. I'd need more than one for a three-day event.

"Of course," he said, leading the way into the cleansing room. "I will ask my aunties to assist you in crafting a few gowns."

"Gowns?"

"You will need them for the evening events."

That's right. At the soiree, I'd also attend the balls, though only to give him guidance, not to find a mate.

I noted the fabricator sitting on a low table, plus the corner cleansing unit and the evacuation pot. I needed to use that soon or my bladder was going to start complaining.

"Feel welcome to fabricate whatever you need," he said. "The unit is programmed to craft almost anything, and there is no cost, especially for something necessary for your position here."

"Thanks." My spine stopped twitching.

In the small room, our closeness hit home. He smelled good despite returning from battle, like mint, the sweet we'd eaten at the end of our meal, plus all male. How did guys do it?

If I'd worked out for ten minutes, my pits would reek, and I'd host a sheen of sweat that would never make me look or smell good.

Nope, I'd resemble a wet rag tossed onto the floor.

"I . . ." His gaze met mine, and I swore his eyes smoldered.

The expression made me feel squirrelly, though in a good way. Like I stood on the top of a building with flying equipment strapped to my back. I was scared but excited. If I stepped off, I might fall and risk a bad injury, or I just might fly.

He nudged forward, pacing after me until my back hit the closed door panel.

I swallowed down a suddenly dry throat. "What were you going to say?" My words squeaked from me.

"Would it be bad to *do* instead of say something?" His voice came out low and husky.

It enthralled me.

"No, it wouldn't," I croaked.

He fingered a band of my hair. "It's soft. Pretty." His gaze traveled to mine. "You are lovely, Kalei." His thumb claw glided down my cheek, stopping at my jaw. He lifted my face so I could do nothing but meet his eyes.

His were *definitely* smoldering.

Butlierflees took flight in my belly again, slamming around with excitement.

"Kalei," he groaned. "I want to kiss you. But after what you told me about your former mate and males on your—"

"Stop talking and kiss me," I breathed.

His mouth slanted across mine, hard and aggressive like

this bold, scarred warrior. His fangs should be sharp against my lips, but they didn't hurt.

The world flipped over as pleasure consumed me. I grabbed onto his muscular forearms to hold myself steady.

He groaned and swept me off my feet, deepening his kiss.

Hunger sparked inside, a raw, needy thing that wouldn't stop making demands until it had been completely satisfied.

There was so much between us. Lust, for sure. Need in spaceship loads. And a feeling of rightness, something I never would've expected.

I'd come here to do a job, but maybe—

Job.

I was here to polish him so he could attract a mate—someone who would *not* be me.

He lifted his head, and I swore I read sorrow in the lines on his face.

I should tell him not to kiss me again, but if he captured my mouth with his, I'd press myself against him and wrap my legs around him and cling.

He slowly lowered me to the floor, my body rubbing against his in a way that heated me up further.

But when my feet reached the ground, he released me and backed away.

My hands dropped to my sides, and the butlierflees in my belly scattered.

"I . . . I will leave your bag outside your door." He shook his head and shifted me to the side so he could open the door. He stepped through the opening and kept going, racing for the platform outside.

I stood in my new bedroom, watching as he opened the outer door and left without saying anything further.

Sighing, I flopped on the bed, groaning at how comfortable it was. Duchess Viola preferred stiff mattresses, and I swore I woke up bruised after the first few nights I'd slept on mine. Was this a section of the mushroom and did it matter?

As for Forje . . . I wasn't sure what to think about him.

Sadly, I had a feeling our kiss was a one-time thing that would never be repeated, and that made my gut clench.

Because I'd just received the kiss of a lifetime.

CHAPTER EIGHT

FORJE

The next morning, I paced the dining room, waiting for Kalei to come downstairs. Assuming she ever would. She may choose to hide in her room after what happened last night.

I'd kissed her. Claimed her mouth with my own.

Our kiss still rumbled through my veins like . . .

Like what?

Ah, yes.

A storm on the plain, sweeping everything up in its path, shaking the strong foundation I'd built for myself.

Yaros ago, I'd settled in this colony with my aunties. I'd planted our wellire and nurtured it. I'd fully expected my aunties to live here while I spent most of my time keeping the Twarvians and other creatures from overrunning the growing community. And after what happened with Shardeene, I assumed I would never mate.

Now I was about to attend a Match-Mating Soiree, and the female I was most interested in would go as my guest, not a potential match.

I had not expected to meet someone who would make me reevaluate everything in life.

For the first time, I was dreaming of my home being more than a stop between battles but instead, a place I ached to return to.

I wasn't sure how I felt about that. I liked Kalei very much, and that was why I'd kissed her. But I couldn't do it again, assuming she agreed to speak with me this dia.

"There you are," she said breezily, striding into the room. Today, she wore a gown she must have fabricated because it wouldn't have fit inside her small bag. Similar to what my aunties wore, though a bit more form-fitting, it hung to just below her knees and puffed around her legs. I liked how it cupped her breasts and dipped down low enough in the front that it showed some of her luscious skin. Two breasts, so unusual when compared to the four possessed by every female in my species.

I dipped my head forward like I would with a commanding officer, realizing right away I knew nothing about how to interact with females. Yes, I'd been with Shardeene, but that was long ago, and it was clear to me now that we'd never communicated well.

An equal number of females to males lived within the colony, but we barely interacted. I saw them on market days when my aunties asked me to shop.

I doubted I should ask Kalei how much she charged for ripe vesilars.

Should I mention the kiss? I'd take my cue from her.

"My aunties have gone to visit friends," I said. "They left food for us, however, and we will eat before we begin lessons, if that is all right with you."

"Of course." She started toward the table.

I hurried to get ahead of her to pull back her chair. Despite my rough manners, solely due to spending most of my time among warriors such as myself, I did absorb teachings well. If I hadn't, I would've been killed in battle by now.

"Thank you," she said as she sat.

She took in the covered platters waiting on the table my aunties had left out. "This looks nice."

I realized how much I appreciated my family's hard effort, something I'd never noted before. They made food. I ate it, often with my hands, while standing beside the counter in the kitchen.

I sat beside her and dragged the covered dishes closer. "Can I serve you your meal?"

"That's very nice of you." She shot me a grin. "You're a quick study. You're going to impress all the females at the Match-Mating Soiree."

What if . . . No, I should not think this way. She was my teacher, not a female I could woo at the soiree.

I shook my head, but it didn't scatter the longing growing inside me.

Maybe if I focused on the task at hand and didn't think too much about what might come next, I could get through this. She'd teach me and soon, we'd leave for the soiree. There, I would meet many females. I'd soon forget about my pretty teacher.

A big part of me shouted no, I never would, but I suppressed the feeling.

I loaded her plate with three slices of salty caracue, two minzir eggs that my aunties had delicately poached, plus two fruit-filled kavia rolls with glistening icing.

"Whoa," she said, placing her hand over her plate. "I've got a great appetite, and everything looks amazing, but if I eat all that, I'll need to curl up on the sofa like a slug and sleep the day away."

"We will walk, and you can teach me polite conversation," I said. "I doubt many females are interested in learning about battle techniques. Plus, we should spend some time with dance." I winced. "I have never danced, and this is a large part of the evening activities at the soiree. The only time I attempted dancing at a prior event, I stepped on my partner's tail so many times that she shrieked and left the dance floor."

Her mood sobered. "She abandoned you in front of everyone? That was mean."

Interesting that she focused on that and not my partner's appendage. "I imagine her tail hurt."

"Still." She stared down at her plate a secunda before looking up. "You're right. We have lots of activities to get through today, and I'll burn off all this food. I'll probably be begging for lunch before we know it." She sucked in a breath and pushed it out. "On behalf of all females, I apologize for her."

"Why? I hurt her, and she was wise to leave me before I did so again."

"I imagine you were embarrassed. I would be."

"Somewhat." No, I'd been mortified. Others had witnessed my defeat, though I'd held my chin up and glared at each person until silence filled the room. Even the musicians stopped playing to watch. I'd made my way to a lounge after that and hadn't returned to the dance floor.

"I'll make sure you feel comfortable this time," she said. "And speaking about various topics. Once we've finished, you'll be the most popular guy at the soiree."

Was it bad that I almost wished I could skip the soiree and spend my time getting to know Kalei instead? My aunties would adamantly say it was. They looked forward to my taking a mate, to having yarlings running about the wellire.

And I did wish to please my aunties.

"Let's eat, then," Kalei said, lifting her dining spire. She held it up. "Today, we only have one, but even at breakfast, there may be more, especially if there's a liquid offering. As I said last night, your best guide is to start from the outside and work your way inward if there's more than one course to the meal."

"Are we allowed to eat any of this with our hands?"

"The sweet kavia bread, yes. No one would expect you to cut it into bite-sized pieces to eat any other way. But definitely do so with the eggs. Since the caracue is crispy strips, I believe it would be all right to eat them delicately with your fingers."

"Not do this, correct?" I said, watching her face to see how she reacted to my tease. I lifted a big slice of caracue and stuffed it into my mouth all at once.

"Definitely." Chuckling, she munched through a small bite, wiggling on her seat and moaning in a way that made my cock twitch again. "Everything is amazing. Your aunts are excellent cooks."

"They are," I pretty much groaned. I needed to get to the soiree soon and find a mate. That was the problem. I hadn't been with anyone in a while. There was no other reason for my cock to be responding so quickly to Kalei.

We finished and took our dishes to the kitchen, where Kalei insisted we wash them.

"Where can we practice dancing?" she asked once we'd finished. "Perhaps we should tackle that before taking a walk. We can combine dancing with polite conversation."

"This way." Should I offer her my arm to walk down the

hall to the open area on one side of the library? Since I wasn't sure, I decided not to touch her. Touch seemed to ignite my skin. At this rate, it would be seared off within dias. I should avoid close contact with her altogether. Once I'd met a tolerable female at the soiree, I would forget all about Kalei.

I urged her ahead of me and into the library.

"Oh, wow. Books! So many books." She hurried across the room and ran her fingers along the spines. "You built cases into the outer mushroom walls."

"Mushroom?"

"Your dwelling looks like a big mushroom to me."

I wasn't sure what a moosh-room was, but I did like how she was stroking the spines of the books I treasured. My stupid body pictured her treating me in just the same manner. She'd have a light touch that would grow firmer as needed. What would her mouth—

No! I needed to stop this. She was here to teach me, not let me back her against the bookcase, strip off her clothing, and run my mouth across every bit of her body.

She turned and leaned against the bookcase. "This is amazing. You even have books in my language."

Imbedded translators allowed us to seamlessly communicate with spoken language. Only a few had upgrades that added reading. Mine was one of them.

"I enjoy reading your language," I said, moving closer to her despite my need to stay away.

"That's cool. What kind of books do you like the most?" As if she was unable to resist, she turned and pulled out one of the English volumes. "Oh, poetry? I love it."

"I . . ."

"What?" She leaned her hip against the bookcase frame

and flipped through the pages. "Emily Dickinson. I'm impressed."

"Why?" I strode so close I could pick up her light, delicate scent that reminded me of enderberries and fresh cloutine. Perhaps she'd asked for her dress to be made of this extra fine, silky fabric. I could picture a strip of it gliding across her—

No!

"Most people," she said, "if they read poetry at all, stick to male poets and the most famous ones."

"Emily Dickinson is famous in your world, is she not?"

"She is." She ran her finger down a page, reading. "I love this one, Why Do I Love You, Sir." Her voice deepened and softened, as if she was afraid of speaking the words aloud. I understood. I felt that way all the time about my own work.

The Sunrise—Sire—compelleth Me—
Because He's Sunrise—and I see—
Therefore—Then—
I love Thee—

She peered up at me through the spikes of hair surrounding her eyes. My species had nothing like them, and I'd noticed them right away. Like her dark hair, I longed to touch those spikes. Were they sharp, tiny weapons to protect her eyes? Or were they as soft as they appeared, as if they'd been placed there to draw my attention and hold it forever?

When she caught me staring, she swallowed, the movement seeming to take a very long time.

"Anyway," she said, lightening her voice. "I'm pleased to see so many books here. Can I . . . Would it be all right for me to borrow them?" Her words rushed out of her. "I promise to take only one at a time, and I'll be careful not to damage them. It's just . . ."

"What?"

"Books are a rarity on Earth now, because paper is so expensive. Everything's electronic, which just isn't the same. A page in a book breathes with a life of its own, don't you think?"

She was not only beautiful and alluring, but we thought alike.

"You can borrow any book you wish and more than one at a time. Enjoy them. I do."

"So, you're the big reader in the house?" She peered up at me, and I read happiness in her eyes. "I don't know why I thought your aunts might be the ones who collected all these books."

"Some are theirs; many are mine. All three of us enjoy reading." Should I tell her about my love of poems? I—

I'd hold off. Too many had laughed at me for me to share now, though I suspected this female might not.

I could compose in my mind; no one would know of this but me.

Light swirled through the air,
touching her sweet profile,
a simple thing that was anything but.

"I guess we should practice dancing," she said, tucking the book of poems close to her chest. "I'll borrow this one first. Thank you."

"You are very welcome." I strode to the dearaphone sitting on a little-used desk and turned it on. "Many of the dances will be fast, but there are slow ones I might be able to . . . well, saying I could master them would sound too confident." I didn't turn to face her. "Please show me how to hold a possible mate in a way that will not harm her?"

"Of course. That's why we're here. I can't promise you'll be the best dancer in the room, but I'm sure I can teach you enough basic steps that you'll feel confident on the dance floor."

"Thank you." I used my wrist com to access the inner dash in the dearaphone, selecting one of the easier tunes. Light music soon filled the room, and I set it to repeat. Even a bit of skill was going to take considerable time to achieve.

"What kind of dancing do the Haehrons do?" she asked.

I shrugged. "I have no true idea. The only time I attempted it, I stepped . . ." She already knew what happened then. "Teach me Earth dancing. I am confident it will suit."

A frowned filled her face. "I'm not sure about that."

"Trust me."

With a pert nod, she held out her arms, and I wished she did that because she wanted to touch me. She did, but not in the way my body—and hearts—longed for.

Light of foot and sweetly dreaming.

I begin where I have never walked before and love . . .

And love . . . *nothing.*

As I stepped close to her, I reminded myself it would be a big mistake to fall in love with my teacher.

CHAPTER NINE

KALEI

"You're tall," I said with a soft laugh, looking up at him.

A teasing smile flitted across his full lips. "You just see this now?"

"The height difference is going to make dancing a challenge."

He scooped me up and spun me around. "Not if I hold you."

I laughed because he was so much fun. My mind spun and not only because he was whirling around. Being held by him reminded me of his kiss, something I'd thought about all night long.

After my restless night, I'd promised myself I'd guard my heart. One touch from Forje, and I tossed my promise aside.

Falling for him would be too easy.

Watching him choose a mate from among the females at the soiree was going to shred me to pieces.

The odd music, a mix of bangs and clanks, soared

through the room as he spun this way and that, a big grin on his face.

"Is this a Haehron dance?" I asked, giddy. My arms were around his neck—I didn't want to fall, now did I? —but keeping myself from falling had nothing to do with the subtle way I stroked his nape.

"It is not," he said, finally coming to a halt. "You are correct. We need to work on Haehron dances."

"I'm afraid I don't know any. Maybe dancing will have to wait until your aunts return?"

"If I can master a simple Earth dance, I could introduce it to a potential mate to intrigue her."

I hated thinking about him intriguing anyone, but this was my job. It would be wrong to cross the line.

"If you put me down, I'll show you a simple waltz. It's a dance Earthlings have done for generations. Other dances come and go in popularity, but the waltz seems to last forever."

When my feet hit the floor, I put my arms around his waist. Our height difference was comical since the top of my head hit about nipple-level on his chest. It reminded me of how silly I was to daydream about being with Forje. I assumed he was big everywhere, which meant there was no way my body could accommodate him during sex.

I took one of his hands and put it around my back then held his other hand outstretched.

"This is a nice, slow dance, and easy to master," I said.

His laugh snorted out. "So you say. Nothing seems to be easy for me to master other than battle."

I peered up at him, taking in the dismay on his face. "If you can battle, that takes quick footwork and finesse, I bet you can waltz as well. Think of it as a smoother form of fighting."

His brow knit, the spikes jutting off the ridgeline quivering. "I will do my best."

"Relax, if you can. You'll enjoy it more."

He grimaced. "I do not believe I will ever enjoy dancing."

We'd see about that.

"Can you get your com to play a waltz?" I asked.

He released my back and lifted his arm. "Let us see."

Soon, the lilting sound filled the room.

Forje's frown deepened. "What is that screeching?"

Funny how enjoyment of music varied from one species to another. "It's a waltz, or close enough to one."

"Should we not practice with the music they will play at the soiree?"

I sighed. "You're right. But bear with me here. I'll teach you with this music playing, then we'll adapt it to yours."

"All right." He agreed readily, but his scowl remained in place as his arm swept across my back again. "Instruct me."

"Think of a box," I said.

"Why would I do that?"

"Four corners. That's where we'll step. If you can keep that in mind, you might actually enjoy this."

"I am having a wonderful time," he said with a scowl.

Sure. I held back my laugh. "It's a popular dance. Really."

He grumbled.

What a grump. A cute grump, however.

"You're the lead dancer," I said.

"This will be interesting."

I pressed on. "There are only six steps for you to remember. The first is to step forward with your left foot, moving your body along with it. After that, you move your right foot to the side."

"Why not forward?"

"Because it goes to the side."

"Very well." If he kept at it, he'd have permanent dents in his forehead.

"Now bring your left foot over and place it beside your right foot."

He did so, his boots creating dull thuds on the squishy floor. "That is only three."

"Hold your horses."

"I do not know what a horse is. Is that the fourth step?"

I chuckled. "Nope. Step back with your right foot, pulling me—gently—along with you. I'll keep up; you don't need to urge me."

"I will need to urge other females who cannot waltz."

"Tell them to follow your lead. I bet by the end of the night; everyone will be waltzing."

"Perhaps."

"The fifth move is to bring your left foot back but complete the square."

He stared down at his feet. "I do not place it next to the right?"

"Once your left foot is spread out to your left, you bring your right foot over next to it. That completes the steps and the box."

"Creating boxes is not dancing."

"It is if we're doing a waltz."

"Very well."

"Let's try it a little faster," I said, tightening my arms around his chest. "Do you want me to lead this one?"

"If it makes you happy."

I rolled my eyes. "Once you've done it a few times, you'll find the waltz is a simple dance. We can move onto

Haehron dances once your aunts return and show me the steps."

"You believe you can master them in a short time?"

"No, but I'm hoping I can become proficient in one or two in time to teach them to you."

"Very well."

"Start the music over again, and we'll waltz a bit."

Soon the lilting music settled within my bones. I'd always loved waltzing; it felt like I was flying.

I led. Forje followed—mostly.

When he stumbled, I did my best to keep him from falling. His tail kept getting in the way, moving forward with his left foot but then tangling with his right. Soon, we were clutching each other and laughing.

"I can see why you find this fun," he said with a grin. "But I believe it would be best for me to *not* offer a waltz to any of the females attending the soiree."

"Give it time. Again."

We continued practicing through the morning, but by the time my belly was starting to rumble, demanding lunch, we were giggling through the dance.

"You're doing very well," I said.

He cocked one side of his brow. "Do your feet agree?"

"They're doing okay. Keep going."

He lifted me up and started waltzing, creating a jerky box but not doing a bad job of it.

"That's it," I cried. "You only need to lift your partner, and you'll impress her."

"Like this?" He dipped forward, taking me with him.

I clung to his shoulders, laughing as he scooped me back up and spun us like a top.

His foot caught on something, and he tumbled backward, taking me with him. We hit the floor and slid across the smooth surface. Like in a romance novel, we came to a stop with me lying on top of him, my thighs straddling his waist.

I braced my chest up with my hands on his shoulders and stared down at him.

Something enormous stirred in his pants, growing hard, thick, and long.

CHAPTER TEN

FORJE

My cock had a mind of its own, and it wanted to be buried within Kalei's body.

I flipped around until she was on the bottom and braced myself over her. Her lips parted with a long sigh, making my cock stiffen further. But her groan of desire made me capture her mouth.

Like I'd dreamed of half the night, I plundered her lips, gliding my tongue inside to stroke hers. I couldn't help it. In everything, I either blundered around or used the finesse I'd gained through battle.

With her, I wanted to feed my fire to her but gently. The last thing I wanted to do was hurt her.

She thrust her hips up, her pelvis hitting my belly.

I left her mouth so I could ease my upper body higher to connect us where I ached for her most.

Her legs wrapped around me and with tiny mews escaping her throat, she ground herself against me.

I was a rocket blasting off the planet and nothing was going to stop me now.

I tugged up her skirt and wrenched the scrap of fabric she wore beneath it aside.

"Yes?" I asked, my voice gritty with need.

"Yes," she cried. "Yes!"

It would be wrong to take her completely. That was what messed things up for me in the past. But I could give her pleasure. There was little harm in that.

I moved down her body until I could reach the juncture between her thighs with my mouth. She smelled amazing and her taste . . .

A groan ripped from me as I glided my tongue through her folds. She was wet already, and the glorious scent of her desire filled the air.

I stroked down her slit, dipping my clawless finger inside before pulling it out so I could lick it.

"Do you want this, Kalei?" I growled. If she said no, I'd stop, though it would be worse than taking a blade to the throat.

"Yes," she whimpered. "I want it."

That was all I needed. I nudged her legs wide and pushed my mouth against her opening, driving my tongue deeply.

She shrieked with pleasure, but this was just the start. Soon, her cries would fill the room. They'd fill my soul.

Her satisfaction is the most seductive thing.

A ripe berry. A warm hearth.

Giving her bliss is my sole desire.

The poem soared within me as I licked her inner walls, savoring her taste while she panted and pressed her hips up to meet my mouth.

She latched onto my horns, holding tight. Her thumbs caressed the tips. My cock slammed against my pants, wanting out, but it would have to wait. It also made the fressars on the tip of my tongue quiver, something I didn't expect. It was said when a Haehron met his fated mate, the fevems sparked within. The spark would travel down the fevems and transmit the sensation to the fated one.

Kalei moaned as my fevems squirmed within her.

She gasped. "Ah, I'm gonna . . ."

I wanted to tell her to let go, to give into the feelings I generated with my tongue, but that would mean leaving her passage. She was too delicious to do something like that.

While I dipped my tongue in and out, the fevems trembled faster, stiffening.

She stroked my horns, and I came undone. I ran my finger through her wet folds, finding the sweet little nub at the top. When I rubbed it, her body quivered. She bucked up to meet my tongue, groaning.

My fevems tightened and released in a rhythmic pattern, sending tiny sparks deep within her. It was said these jolts would help prepare a mate to receive a male's seed and ensure they took hold. I didn't know about that, but I knew that driving Kalei wild with pleasure brought me deep satisfaction.

I licked deeper, rubbing my fevems against her upper wall.

Her cries echoed in the small room, each one making my cock twitch. I was going to come from that alone, and nothing would make me feel better.

Her breathing grew ragged, and her body tightened.

I continued to stroke her inner walls and rub her sweet bud while she came apart beneath me.

Her body went limp. I gently eased my tongue from her slick passage and grinned up at her.

I was about to speak when voices rang out in the hall.

"Forje?" Auntie Enzia called.

"Kalei? I wonder where they are?" Aunt Rozen said.

"I believe we should look in the library, sister."

"Oh, yes, do let us go to the library. I hear music. Perhaps they are still practicing dancing, and we can watch."

Kalei's panicked gaze met mine.

I backed off, rising to my feet and tugging her up beside me. She quickly straightened her clothing, but nothing could be done for her pink cheeks and messed hair.

"Ah, there you are," Aunt Rozen said as she strode into the room with Enzia right behind.

"I see you have been dancing. Kalei, you look stressed." She shot me a scowl. "You haven't been stepping on her tail, have you, great-nephew?"

"I don't have a tail, so no," Kalei said in a limp voice.

"Her toes might be sore, but I believe I am mastering the waltz," I said. Mastering Kalei as well, but nothing would induce me to speak the words. Not until we were alone.

She sagged against me, and the soft smile on her face pierced my hearts. I'd put that satisfied look there. I'd brought her pleasure.

She walks with the grace of the fleetest pellafleur,

her lips brighter than the ripest ruspisette berries.

Kalei was my fated mate. My fressars proved it even if my hearts hadn't already known.

This female would bring me my greatest joy in life once I'd claimed her.

Assuming she wanted to be claimed.

Could she be persuaded to be my only one? I didn't need a Match-Mating Soiree to find a mate, not while she resided within my wellire already.

She'd welcomed my tongue into her body and my kisses. That had to mean something.

If I had any say in it, this would not be the last time I'd touch her.

CHAPTER ELEVEN

KALEI

I'd just had the best orgasm in my life, and it hadn't involved a driving cock. I wasn't sure what to think about it.

Rich had never done anything like that.

It wasn't fair to compare guys, but I did. Rich . . . was not a lover but a taker, and his needs had been what mattered most.

But Forje . . . Would we have done more if his aunts hadn't walked in? I wasn't sure what to think about that, either.

Nothing at the moment. Thinking would only make me blush in front of Enzia and Rozen, and they'd ask questions.

"We were about to . . . get some lunch," I said. "Right Forje?" I couldn't look up at him. An odd vulnerability filled me. I'd had sex with guys other than Rich. I'd felt pleasure much like this before, though never from only a tongue. His had to be magic because I'd sworn it released sparks deep within me.

I wanted to feel it again, but that path was forbidden.

He was my boss, for heaven's sake. As for his aunts? It was all I could do to look them in the eye.

Not only that, Forje was about to attend an event that would help him pick out a mate.

Not me. He'd never want to mate with his human teacher.

That thought sliced pain through me, and I struggled to shove the feeling aside as I tightened my spine and followed them from the library and to the kitchen, Forje politely stopping beside each door and gesturing for me to go ahead of him.

"If you do not mind," Enzia said as she urged us to the small stools at the butcher block in the middle of the room. "We could dine here for this meal and be ready again for a formal multi-course repast for dinner."

"That's fine," I said. I could barely think. There was no way I'd have the wits to instruct Forje in dining etiquette right now. I needed a nap or time away from him to think and regroup. Even more, I had to find a way to shove aside my growing feelings for him.

"I thought after lunch, if you can spare the time," Enzia said to me as she removed covered dishes from the chiller and placed them on the counter. They must've prepared them earlier and put them aside. A quick zap in the regenerator heated them, and yummy smells soon filled the air. "We could help you with a few gowns for the soiree."

"Indeed, sister," Rozen said, setting the table for four.

I jumped in to help while Forje watched me. What was he thinking? Did he have regrets? I should, but I couldn't seem to grab onto them and make them mine. No, all I wanted to do was kick his aunts from the kitchen, climb onto the table and lift my skirt, then beckon him closer. I was addicted to his sparking tongue.

"Kalei will be lovely dressed in Haehron finest," Rozen said.

"What color do you think?" Enzia asked her.

"Pink, naturally." She stroked the bodice of her fuchsia gown. I'd noticed she wore pink the day before and Enzia blue—she was dressed in blue again today. If they kept this up, I'd always be able to tell them apart.

"Blue as well. One cannot wear pink to all the events," Enzia said. "And if you like, we could have one made in yellow."

Rozen nodded. "White, too."

"The soiree only lasts three dias," I said, settling on a stool. "Are there dances each night?"

"Yes, of course," Rozen said. She and her sister sat with me and Forje on the opposite side. She lifted the covers off the dishes, revealing enough food for a Haehron army. "Please," She handed me a serving spoon, "take whatever you would like. I, for one, am hungry after walking to and from the market."

"You didn't take a skimmer?" I asked.

Her head cocked to the side. "Why would I do that when my legs still work, and my body is healthy?"

"We have a skimmer, but we park it on the edge of town with the others," Forje said. "The wellires don't like having ships nearby. It is all they can do to tolerate the devices we bring inside, like the fabricator."

"And the chiller," Rozen said with a chuckle. "This wellire started whipping back and forth when it saw us approach. Only Forje's tender touch and communion with it made it settle."

"I thought it was a regular old plant," I said. "I didn't realize it could think."

"Wellires live for many Haehron lifetimes," Enzia said,

dishing up food for herself. She lifted an eating implement and scooped up a bite. "We will not be the first to shelter within its walls."

"Is it watching us?" I asked, struggling not to cringe. What I meant was, did it watch me and Forje in the library?

"Why would it do something like that?" Rozen asked.

"No," Forje said. "It watches outside but not within the inner walls."

That was a relief.

"What's it like to commune with a wellire?" I asked, curious about the enormous plant. To think an entire species lived inside them.

"It is the solemn duty of the eldest in the family," Rozen said.

I took a bite and spoke after swallowing. "Wouldn't that be one of you?"

"Normally, but Forje is the eldest of his direct line. We wanted to live with him when we settled in this colony, so we are happy he took care of the wellire. It makes more sense for him to help it grow than us, since he will live longer."

It made me sad to think they'd die. They were sweet, funny ladies. "I hope that won't be for a long time."

"Fate has a way of snatching people from their lives," Rozen said. "But I intend to live long enough to see Forje's yarlings."

Enzia nodded pertly. "Very true, sister. Me as well."

We ate, and I helped them clean up afterward, Forje disappearing from the kitchen, mumbling something about duties to attend to in his office.

"Now, we go to the fabricator," Enzia said, clapping her hands and hopping.

"Pink first, sister," Rozen said, hurrying to the opening

leading to the hall. "Come along, Kalei. Our largest fabricator is located in my bedroom."

Enzia scowled as we reached the foyer and started up the stairs. "I don't know why you got the largest one. As the eldest, it should've gone to me."

"Because you only wear blue, sister."

"And you only wear pink," Enzia said.

Rozen stroked her dress. "It is the prettiest color; don't you agree Kalei?"

There was no way I was getting into the middle of that. "I love both. Maybe each of you can select a gown in your favorite color? I'll wear a different one each night."

"A splendid idea," Enzia said.

Rozen linked her arm through mine, tugging me into one of the rooms on the opposite side of the hall from mine. Which room was Forje's?

I didn't need to know. It wasn't like I'd be tiptoeing to his room late at night.

Maybe not.

Jeez. I needed to stop thinking about him that way. He'd never be mine.

"You'll wear my gown the first night, correct, Kalei?" Enzia asked.

Ugh. I couldn't choose one over the other; it wouldn't be fair. "Why don't we make one gown that's pink and blue," and hopefully not hideous, "and then I can wear both your favorite colors on the first night. I'll select some colors for the other evenings, like green, black, or maybe white." The last would look great with my dark hair. Speaking of which . . . "How do females wear their hair here? You two have yours pulled up today but yesterday, you wore it down."

"In addition to your room on the space station, we have arranged for someone to help you with your face and hair," Rozen said, guiding me over to the big fabricator taking up one wall. Small units were great for simple things like shirts and pants, but for a gown like I imagined—a-la-Cinderella—we'd need to use the larger unit.

"Do females wear make-up to events like this?" I asked, perching on the edge of one of the two beds. The sisters had adjoining rooms spanning the entire length of this side of the hall.

"They do," Enzia said. "I am not sure what they will do for your face to help you fit in, but they are the masters. They will understand what is needed."

Now I was a bit nervous about this. "It won't be simple make-up like what you're wearing now?" Assuming they were wearing any. I couldn't tell.

Enzia patted my arm. "You shall see."

They strode over to the fabricator.

"Pink *and* blue? It must be pretty," Enzia said.

"No, it will be *blue* and pink, sister," Rozen said. She started pressing buttons and beeps rang out.

Enzia nudged her aside and pressed more buttons. "*Pink* and blue."

I sighed as the device started humming. A ping and the door opened, revealing a gown unlike anything I'd seen before in my life.

"I do say, sister," Enzia exclaimed. "It is lovely."

Rozen nodded. "It truly is."

"Is that the back of it?" I asked, sliding off the bed and crossing the room to join them.

"Oh, no, it is the front," Enzia said, tugging it from the device. "Sister, we need to help her make a few more gowns, and then it will be time to pack. She leaves tomorrow afternoon for the space station with Forje!"

"But, but . . ." I struggled not to cringe as I gaped at the dress. "My boobs are going to hang out."

CHAPTER TWELVE
FORJE

The minue I reached my office, I commed my commanding officer.

"Ah, Forje," he said cheerfully. "Ready to return to the frontline so soon?"

"I did not call you for that. Actually . . ."

"What?"

"What if I wanted to resign my commission?"

He grumbled. "You are joking, correct?"

"What if I am not?"

A long pause followed. "You have served a long time. If you wish to sever your commission, you are welcome to do so. I will say that we will miss you. Few have your skills in battle."

"It is something I have been thinking of," I said.

"I see. Perhaps you should take more time to think, then?"

Perhaps I should. I enjoyed battling. I was needed. I didn't have to resign yet.

"Take the rest of your time off and let me know when

you return," he said. "You do not need to come to this decision now."

"You are right."

"As always," he said with a chuckle. He ended the call, and I slumped in my chair.

Think. It seemed I did more thinking now than I had during my entire life.

What was I going to do about Kalei?

She was my fated mate, and I had no idea how to handle it. My aunties expected me to select a Haehron female from among those attending the soiree. They did not expect me to come home and announce I wanted to mate with my teacher instead. Assuming my teacher wished to mate with me. Despite charging into battle without a speck of fear, I found my guts shaking when I contemplated Kalei's rejection.

Sure, she'd kissed me, and she'd let me stick my tongue inside her passage—a memory that made me hard whenever I thought about it—but that didn't mean she wanted to be with me for more than a minue.

Fate is a wondrous, sad thing.

If love persisted, so did your heart.

But if it didn't . . .

I didn't want to think about what might happen then. I was hurt when Shardeene rejected me. I'd be devastated if Kalei did.

Wait—love? I couldn't be falling in love with Kalei. Yet . . . What if I was?

Well, then I'd do my best to return from the Match-Mating Soiree with a mate, but she would be Kalei.

We practiced more dancing through the afternoon, and I watched her. She seemed happy to be with me, but was she pretending? Maybe she smiled at me because I was her student and she, my teacher. This might only be a job for her. Teachers didn't often let students shove their tongue inside her passage or give her kisses, but this wasn't the normal student-teacher interaction. We were adults, not yarlings.

I was still pondering what to do about my growing feelings as I said goodnight to her that evening.

"Tomorrow we will travel to the space station," I said, struggling to find a way to continue the conversation. She'd been strangely quiet all evening, focusing solely on my instruction at the dining room table and then teaching me polite conversation after.

"In the afternoon."

"Yes. Once we are there, I will escort you to your quarters. Please remain there unless I accompany you. It isn't safe for a female to wander around alone on the space station." The thought of anything happening to her made my hearts come to a shuddering halt. "I will protect you," I hastened to add. "Never doubt this."

She placed her hand on my forearm. "I know, Forje. You won't let anything bad happen to me."

Her words made my hearts start beating again.

"Most of the activities will take place within the same area on the station, and our quarters will be located nearby. There will be no reason for you to seek other sections of the station." Where she would endanger herself.

She cocked her head and her eyes sparkled. "What if I want to go sightseeing or buy souvenirs?"

I frowned. "Why would you wish to do anything like that?"

"Maybe I need a T-shirt that says I was there?"

"T . . .?"

Her smile faded, though her eyes still gleamed with humor. "It's an inside joke, I guess. If I want to wander around a bit, will you go with me? There must be free time during the soiree."

"Yes, there is, and yes, I will walk with you wherever you wish to go. Perhaps we could go to the market."

"Yes!" Her eyes stopped sparkling. "Unless you're busy with whoever you choose as a mate."

"You assume someone would be willing to mate with me." Even if I didn't want Kalei, I wasn't sure it was possible for me to woo a mate.

"Who wouldn't want to be with you?"

Who indeed. What if I told her I wanted her?

It was too soon. I had the dias of the soiree to court her. Woo her, as my aunties had suggested. I didn't know what they'd think if I brought her home and presented her to them as my mate—assuming she agreed.

But I was going to do all I could to show Kalei she was mine.

KALEI

"Showing your breasts is very popular right now," Callaloo said. She stroked her bright blue hair with one of her four arms.

The aunties had arranged for her services for the duration of the soiree, and she'd arrived at my room not long after we landed on the space station. I'd barely unpacked before she'd descended to fix my hair, face, and, evidently, my boobs.

I tried to hike up the bodice that skimmed below my boobs, projecting them upward, but there would never be enough material to cover my nips.

"If you let me attach the nipple ornaments I brought, you'll fit right in." She held up the dangly things with clips on the top.

"Nope," I said, covering my poor nipples. "I don't want to stride around with them taking in the view. And besides, I'm here to help Forje, not find a mate."

She wiggled her four eyebrows—dyed as blue as her long, straight hair. "Attending the Match-Mating Soiree is the opportunity of a lifetime. I cannot believe you would attend without taking the chance to find a mate." Her grin widened, showing off her two-inch tusks. "Even if you only mate with him for the duration of the soiree."

I frowned. "Do people do that? I thought this event was for finding a lifelong mate, not hook-ups."

"Hooking up or down can be amazing." She advanced toward me with the nipple ornaments lifted. "At least see how they look before dismissing them and taking a prudish stance by covering your breasts."

I was all for fitting in, but how could I look Forje in the eye with my boobs hopping around between us?

Turning partway away from her, I held out my hand. "Let me have them. I'll put them on."

"Very well." She watched while I did so.

At least they didn't pinch.

Callaloo sighed. "I promise, everyone is going to ohh and ahh when you make your appearance at the ball."

Yeah, because they could peek at my tits.

A light snack had been brought to the room, and the steward who delivered it cautioned me to leave room in my belly for the evening buffet. I picked at it.

Why bother showing my boobs at all? My heart ached because it was going to be tough watching Forje flirt and dance with all the other females while I hung out by the wall, watching. How could I smile and tell him I was happy for him when he and the lucky female announced they were mating?

"No sad face," Callaloo said, tapping my chin. "You will mess up my hard work. Smile, lovely one. Never fear. With the ornaments, you will attract many males. Or females if that is what you prefer."

I only wanted Forje, who was very much male. I wasn't sure when I'd started falling in love with him, though I guessed it was somewhere between him raving about the books in his library and driving his electric tongue deep inside me. Why the two were a toss-up was beyond me. Any guy who could make me come with his tongue and a few strokes of his finger was mating material in my book. But seeing him treasure poetry had struck something deep inside me. It wounded me, though in a good way, and I wouldn't be healing anytime soon.

She continued to primp, straightening my dress and adding more color to my face.

"Look now," Callaloo said, turning me to face the smooth surface of the wall that served as a decent mirror. "Lovely, am I right?"

Whoa. "That's not me." If I didn't know better, I'd think a total stranger stared back at me—a beautiful stranger.

"Yes, it's you. You are gorgeous, Kalei. The males will be stomping toward you, demanding you dance with them alone."

I hoped they were interested in the waltz, then, because I had no clue how to do alien dances.

I took in my upswept hair and the crushed stone she'd coated my upper eyelids with—all the way to my eyebrows —plus the thick lash-coating she'd applied to my lashes. The blue and pink gown with a high waist and a flaring skirt that brushed the tops of my feet outlined my curves, making them look great. The colors were surprisingly pleasing, and I felt good other than my boobage hanging out.

Thankfully, the ornaments didn't pinch, and they did cover my nips. The sparkly material flared out around the clips like shooting stars, and the dangly bits covered part of my big boobs.

"You promise everyone will be dressed like this?" I asked, on the fence about it.

"I promise." Callaloo tapped her forehead with two fingers. "Everyone will be speaking about you tonight. Such lovely hair—so different from those in attendance. And your exquisite face! I have only enhanced it, not overly coated it, don't you think?"

"I look amazing." Turning, I spontaneously hugged her.

She wiggled and sighed, but I sensed she was happy I showed her how pleased I was in this way.

"I must leave now, but you are ready," she said. "The male you arrived with will be very impressed."

That would be wonderful. Almost worth showing off my nips.

"Forje isn't with me. We're just friends." Sorta. Friends with benefits, I supposed. Although, I was the only one benefitting from the arrangement so far. From what I could tell, he'd still had a raging hard on after I'd come.

"He did not look at you as if you were friends."

She had to be mistaken.

"He's here to find a mate, but it won't be me. I'm here as his teacher. I instructed him in etiquette."

"And came to care for him while you did so, am I not right?"

Damn, she was perceptive. Could everyone see? She must be mistaken about Forje.

"Thank you so much," I said. "I look good because of your efforts."

"You shine. Don't forget that." She patted my back. "Are you ready to go? I will take you to the entrance."

"I just need my shoes."

Enzia and Rozen had fabricated shoes as well, elfishappearing things with curled up, pointed toes. Only the bells were missing.

With my clutch in hand, I left my small room with Callaloo.

The hall was narrow, but on the station, space went for a premium price. I could only imagine how expensive my room must cost for one night.

As we'd approached the space station, I'd been in awe of the stars around us. Planets gleamed in the distance, and lights flickered along the enormous, multi-level structure that resembled a cruise ship from Earth's past. We'd docked, and Forje led me through numerous metal hallways, up levels via elevators, and finally through a network of alleys before stopping in about the middle of the ship. He'd made sure my room was locked and I felt secure before leaving for his own quarters.

We passed a few portholes, showing us walking along the outside wall of the ship, and I spied more shuttles coasting closer. The station was busy.

"How many people will attend the soiree?" I asked Callaloo.

"Hundreds."

"That many?" Trepidation crept up my spine. I'd be lost in the ballroom. If I didn't find Forje, how was I going to help him? I paused at a small window, staring out while trying to ground myself and control my nerves. Two moons orbited around a distant, pale blue planet with darker landmasses, and even more ships soared toward the space station.

"We are almost there," Callaloo said, pausing beside me to give me a once-over. She tucked a stray strand of hair back into my upswept arrangement, then slowly nodded approval. "You still appear lovely." Her smile made my nerves stop twitching. "I would tell you not to worry, that you will enjoy this, but each must come to this realization on their own."

"I'm nervous," I said, my hands fidgeting at my sides. "I guess you can tell."

"It is understandable. Know that you are dressed in the latest fashion and that your hair and make-up are perfect. You will shine partly because you are so different." She tapped my arm. "Trust me in this."

"You're right. I feel good because you helped me look fantastic." I sucked in a deep breath and tried not to watch my boobs shifting around from the effort. "I'm ready."

"Ready to impress everyone inside that room?" She pointed to a big set of double doors waiting on the opposite side of the big room ahead. Aliens dressed in their finest mingled in the open area while others strode confidently through the crowd and entered what looked like an enormous ballroom, if my quick peek was any indication.

Butlierflees skipped around in my belly, making me grateful I'd only nibbled on the snack. There was nothing worse than going to a party all by yourself. Sure, Forje would be here, but he had come to meet females, not entertain me.

I really was going to hang out in a corner—facing the corner so my boobs wouldn't show.

"I will leave you here, then," Callaloo said. "You will be safe among the crowd. Do not go off with anyone without telling someone else where you will be."

Yes, Mom.

Really, though, she was right. "Thank you. I won't."

She shook a finger my way. "Do not take a drink from someone else. Always obtain it from a server or the bar."

"Drugged drinks are almost older than time."

"It is wise to be cautious."

"Yes, you're right." My teeth chattered as a few females dressed much like me passed. One displayed four breasts, each with an ornament much like mine. Seeing them walking with their chins high made my spine stop quivering. My legs still shook, but knowing I'd fit in helped. "Thank you again."

She braced my shoulders once before leaving me to take on the Match-Mating Soiree.

I opted to hang out in the hall for now, watching as others arrived and went inside. From the calls in the ballroom, it appeared someone was announcing each of the guests. Would they do that for me? I was the hired help, so I'd probably slink inside. Everyone would stare at me for a second, before looking away. At least that would allow me to hurry into a dark corner where I could hide.

"Excuse me," someone said from behind me.

I turned to find an Earth woman dressed in a cop's outfit trying to get past me. Tall and curvy, she'd coiled her amber hair into a big tight bun at her nape. She shot me a stilted smile. "I'm running a bit late."

"Didn't you hear? We're supposed to let our boobs hang out." I didn't know why I said it. She just seemed . . . nice, despite her stiff demeanor.

She paused, her eyebrows lifting. "Excuse me?" Her gaze sped down my front. "Oh. Ha." Her bright laugh slipped out, softening her tight posture. "It takes some getting used to, doesn't it? The first time I saw someone dressed like that, and with six breasts, I might add, it was all I could do not to stare. But if you're nervous about exposing yourself, don't be. You'll fit right in." She tapped her chest. "As for me, I'm working so I get to cover up."

"I imagine I'll get used to it." Or I wouldn't. For the rest of the soiree, I'd fabricated more modest styled gowns, using a mix of Haehron fashion and what I remembered from vids of award ceremonies back on Earth.

She nudged my upper arm. "If you want, walk in with me. They're not used to female police, so I'll draw some of the attention."

"You're working tonight?"

Her spine tightened again, and a sharp look filled her pretty green eyes. "I'm the head of security for the event."

"Congratulations. I bet you're doing an amazing job."

Her eyes softened. "Thanks. As long as everyone listens to me, things should go fine."

"You don't expect trouble, do you?"

She shrugged. "You can never tell during an event like this. Last yaro, two males fixated on one female, and she couldn't decide who she preferred. It turned into a brawl in the middle of the dancefloor, and I had to break it up. Another time, a few creatures arrived on the station as stowaways. They made a mess of the buffet before I could escort them to a ship that would take them back to where they'd come from."

"Wow. Sounds like you might be busy, after all."

"You're the one who'll be busy." A smile flashed across her lips before her mouth smoothed. "We don't see many Earthlings here, let alone anyone with only two breasts. You might find yourself the belle of the ball."

There was only one guy I wanted to attract, and that wasn't happening.

"I just hope I don't stand out in a bad way," I said.

"You won't. Trust me."

"Thank you." Speaking with her helped me relax. "Maybe if I enter with you, like you said, I won't feel such a wreck."

"All right, then." She held out her hand. "I'm Charlotte, but you can call me Charlie. Everyone does."

She tugged me toward the doors. We stopped outside, and her hand reached for the knob.

"Ready to make a splash?" she asked.

I chuckled wildly before tightening my spine. "I'm going to pretend I'm excited and not a total wreck."

"That's the best way to do it."

Voices rose and fell inside the room ahead.

"Is there anyone waiting for you inside?" she asked.

Forje must be surrounded by females by now. He wouldn't notice I was here, though it was nice to dream he would.

"No, but I'm sure I'll meet a few guys," I said bravely.

"Then let's do it." She opened the doors and strode inside.

I hurried into the huge ballroom behind her.

CHAPTER FOURTEEN

FORJE

I knew the minue Kalei walked into the enormous ballroom.

I *felt* her presence.

When my fressar flares on my tongue started throbbing, emitting tiny sparks, I clamped my mouth shut and watched her pause in the big open doorway. My jaw dropped, and I was sure I looked stupid with my mouth open and tiny sparks falling to the floor, but she looked amazing.

Another Earth woman dressed in security clothing walked in with her, quickly leaving her after a touch on Kalei's arm.

Kalei wore a blue and pink gown that made her skin glow like the rarest juliest. As was Haehron fashion, the garment exposed her chest, and I gaped at the pale skin of her two breasts broken only by gleaming silver ornaments attached to her nipples.

Her hair had been swept up, revealing her delicate neck, and Callaloo had done something with Kalei's face that made her look even prettier than I remembered.

Her gaze scanned the room and landed on me.

Heat flared in my chest, and I wanted to rush across the big ballroom, take her hand, and tell her she was the most gorgeous being I'd seen in my life. Tell her I wanted her as my mate and no one else.

But I wasn't sure what she thought of me. Did she see me in the same way? So far, loving her with my tongue hadn't ruined what we'd started but it had with Shardeene.

Instead of bellowing her name and stomping over to her, I walked carefully in her direction, in the way she'd instructed. *No galloping. No stomping your feet.*

A few humans and many aliens from a variety of species shifted around me. Some of the females danced to the light music playing, while others stood in clusters near the tables, picking through the platters of food. Yet others stood in line for beverages from the bar.

Such strange concepts, a buffet and a bar. They'd been brought here from Earth. No one did anything like it where I or most of the other alien males came from. But from the time the space station was commissioned, those who settled here first built structures catering to a wide variety of people, Earthlings among them.

Frankly, this ballroom humbled me. I'd grown up in a small town and in an equally small wellire. It was only my experience in our military that gained me a loftier position in our colony, plus a wellire seed that would grow a large residence. Many were much smaller within my community.

Tonight, males made up the majority of the guests, and many of us had only a vague idea about how to court females.

From what I could tell, only two matches had been made so far this evening.

Quite a few males stood near the wall on my right,

looking decidedly uncomfortable. They either stared wide-eyed at the females dancing or the food. A few gulped, and I suspected they were getting up the nerve to approach a female, though I wasn't confident they would.

While the human security guard stepped down the stairs and started working her way around the room, her hand on the hilt of her weapon strapped to her waist, Kalei gaped at the crowd. Earlier, I'd gawked at the tall ceilings and window flanking one side of the room, looking out at the stars.

A Vestulian male dressed in the same uniform as the servers joined Kalei and spoke to her in a low voice. She swallowed and said something, making him nod.

He turned to face the audience and cleared his throat. "From Earth, I present Kalei Bridget Sutherland."

A few males frowned while others started toward her. If I didn't get to her quickly, she'd be claimed.

I picked up my pace, the rule for not stomping or running be damned. I'd reach her first and then, at least, she'd know she had a known choice beyond the offerings of strangers.

What should I say to her? Oh, wait. Would it be bad to ask for instruction? I actually felt confident now. I knew how to eat without embarrassing myself, and I could avoid dancing.

At the bottom of the stairs, I stopped, staring up at her. Other males crowded behind me, watching to see if I'd approach her and claim her.

My heart thundered in my chest, and my spine kept twitching.

Did I dare try to speak to her about something other than polite conversation and protocols?

I *had* to. If I didn't help her see I was someone she could love, someone else would step between us and steal her away.

With my nerves on fire, I started up the steps.

She waited at the top, looking at me. Did I spy relief in her eyes?

One step more and . . .

I tumbled forward, crashing to the floor at her feet.

CHAPTER FIFTEEN

KALEI

When Forje fell at my feet, someone snickered. A few of the females standing nearby in the ballroom outright laughed.

Fury heated my face to a boiling point, and I shot a glare at those still snickering. When I caught their eye, they looked down at the floor. Silence filled the room.

I stooped down beside Forje, placing my hand on his shoulder. "Are you all right?"

"I am well," he groaned. He rose to sit on the top step and rubbed his face with both palms. "You tried so hard to teach me social graces, and I wanted to absorb your every word, but I was not successful."

"We only had two days."

"Nonetheless, I . . . I apologize."

"It's not your fault."

"I . . ." His tail coiled around his legs, and I got the idea he wished he could hide. I'd feel the same if it happened to me.

I sat beside him on the steps. "So, this is quite the soiree."

"Excuse me?"

He wouldn't look at me. Should I have ignored his fall?

"If anyone understands what it's like to be embarrassed in front of others, it's me," I said in a light tone. Thankfully, those around us had gone back to dancing or standing in line at the bar and buffet table.

"What are you speaking of?" he said with a frown. When he did that, his entire face scrunched, even the thick unibrow marching across his forehead. The little spike that I actually found entertaining wiggled.

"Do you have time for a little story?" I asked.

"Always."

That was sweet of him, especially when he was here to find a mate, not sit and chat with me. I took a deep breath and shoved out the words. "When my parents died and I moved in with my aunt, they sent me by shuttle."

"How old were you?"

"Fourteen."

"Old enough to make adult decisions, yet young enough to feel you are still a child."

"Yup. The shuttle landed on the edge of town, near where they'd set up a fair. There were tons of people there, and many looked toward the shuttle, probably wondering what in the world was going on. I walked down the ramp of the ship—"

"Gangplank," he said.

I tipped my head his way. "Hmm?"

"You walked down the *gangplank*."

"Okay, but that's not the point of the story."

He stared at me in what appeared to be fascination, like I was a new specimen on display in a lab. "I apologize. Please continue."

"When I got to the bottom of the *gangplank*, it was hot

outside. I stopped and yanked my sweater up over my head. My shirt rode up, and I wasn't wearing a bra." I peered down at my exposed chest. "Trust me, on Earth, no one dresses like this. Showing your boobs is considered embarrassing."

"You were upset."

"Very."

His gaze shot to my breasts. "Who saw this? I will kill them for you."

My laugh burst out. "Then? I would've been all over the idea. I've learned to shrug it off, though. As you can see, I've had a complete change in point of view. Look at me, letting my breasts hang out other than for these," I flicked one of them, "sparkly ornaments covering my nips."

"Did everyone who was watching shrug this off?"

"Um, mostly. After a while." At the time, every guy within a quarter mile stared, their gazes branding my bare flesh. They'd kept staring whenever I dared to show my face in town after that. Some sought me out, asking me to take walks with them. To eat with them. To flash my boobs at them. "I was just a freakin' kid, but if your body grows up before you feel like an adult inside, every guy out there thinks you can be his."

Knowing what they'd seen made me shudder at their advances.

"I do not believe you should belong to anyone but yourself," he vowed.

"Thank you."

"What did you do?" he asked.

"I yanked down my shirt and tried to scoot behind a couple other women, but . . ."

"But what?"

"Some of them laughed too."

"I will kill them all," he snarled, peering around. "Who first?"

I chuckled, placing a restraining hand on his muscular forearm that was as gorgeous and muscular as the rest of him. "Don't kill anyone for me. Truly. It's over. Almost everyone has forgotten, and even if they haven't, none of them are here."

He watched my face. "Have *you* forgotten?"

"Mostly."

"I sense this still bothers you."

"At least no one in your village knows about it. It's in the past. Heck, it was half my lifetime ago. I should've been able to put it behind me. My point was, I understand being embarrassed, and I imagine you can move past this quickly." Easy to say, not so easy to do. Me being a perfect example of that.

"I slammed onto the floor at your feet," he said. "Like when I tripped over the plant at a prior event, I am truly embarrassed."

"Then maybe we need to do something about it?" I asked.

His thick brow scrunched, his majestic horns shifting with the action. They curled up over his head, and they were thick. The kind of horns a girl wanted to grab onto when the guy . . .

I squirmed, my body suffusing with desire. It was time to put that steamy image from my mind.

He tipped his head up and sniffed the air. "Something smells marvelous."

Ugh. I was going to melt into the floor if he said he could smell my arousal.

"How do you suggest we make everyone forget I crashed onto the floor?" he asked, his nose wrinkling and his eyes scanning the area, seeking the source of the aroma.

"We could do something together, something loud and fun, and that will distract them."

"Ah," he said. "Would you like to play bungafleer?"

"What's bungafleer?"

"A common activity among my people." He turned a gaze full of humor my way. "I believe it would be best to show you."

CHAPTER SIXTEEN

FORJE

After I'd tumbled to the ground at her feet, I was strangely humbled that she hadn't laughed like the others. Instead, only concern and sympathy filled her pretty eyes.

Hurt came through in her voice when she told her story, and her gaze had sought other females within the room, telling me she'd been betrayed when they laughed back then, and those here in this room that mocked me reminded her of that minue.

At least Kalei wasn't running away from me.

I climbed to my feet and held my hand out to her. "Which shall it be? We could dance or walk in the gardens instead of playing bungafleer?"

"Since it's a common game where you come from," she said, taking my hand. "Let's play bungafleer."

I dipped my head forward.

We strode through the room, and I didn't feel one bit of embarrassment for my fall because Kalei was with me. I'd come to the match-mating event but only to woo her.

Leaving the main ballroom, we took the hall to the end and entered the room they'd set aside for games.

"Oh." She stopped in the open doorway. "Look at all the little creatures leaping and running around."

I took in the tables set up with various games, each hosted by a staff member hired by the soiree committee. Within the circular tables, various tiny mechanical creatures scampered about. Others battled, while at nearby tables, they completed intricate obstacle courses.

Did she see how fun this could be? We'd brought this game and the game pieces from my home planet to the colony, and even though other species had moved there as well, growing their own wellires to live in, all of them played bungafleer. Here, I noted many species enjoying the game, though few humans played.

Perhaps they danced or ate and would join later?

Kalei watched for a few moments before shooting me a smile. "Which game is bungafleer?"

I pointed to the tables along the right wall. "The competitors are bungafleer, and they are robotic, not true creatures. Over here," I directed her to a table along the right wall where she could build her bungafleer to compete with.

"I don't understand, "she said when I handed her a torso. "What do I do with it?"

"I start with arms." I lifted two with claws on the ends and attached them to my gaming torso.

"I do like arms."

Heat suddenly flared in my groin, and my cock stirred. Why was I excited because she said she liked arms?

Because she was staring at mine as if she wanted to lick them.

"Legs, too." My voice came out husky. "You will need . . . legs."

She searched my face. "Legs can be pretty awesome as well."

My cock smacked against the front of my pants, and I was grateful the table hid my growing erection from view. She was not discussing sex. I should not be thinking, let alone dreaming of sex, despite how close we'd come to sharing it the other day.

"A head." Why couldn't I speak without feeling short of breath? I had not run or battled anyone.

"Head." She popped one onto the neck of her torso. "I want two, I think."

We finished building our bungafleer and turned. I solemnly prayed no one looked our way or noticed how my cock prodded the front of my pants. *Calm down,* I told it. *You have no reason to do this.*

I knew why it did it. Kalei was the only person I dreamed of. My mate. My goal was to claim her before the end of the soiree.

But getting her into my bed was not an option for the foreseeable future. I would court her and after enough time had passed, and I was confident she liked me and our goals were the same, I would ask her to be my mate.

"Once we have finished constructing our competitors, we can enter them in the events," I said.

She turned with her long-legged bungafleer dangling from her hand. "Our bungafleer has to make it through each event?"

"Only the ones you choose to enter."

She winced when a bungafleer at one of the tables clambered up onto the side and dove to the floor, shattering on impact. Its alien handler groaned and flung up his four hands.

"Oh," she said, staring down at her bungafleer lying across her hand. "Are you sure they don't somehow come alive?"

"They are not. Once they are completed, we turn them on." I showed her the switch at the back of the neck. "Only then can they function. They are not harmed if they . . . fall."

"All right, then," she said, her gaze sly. "This might be fun. What's the prize if my robot wins?"

"Happiness?"

She laughed and placed her hand on my arm, lowering her voice. "No, really, what's the prize?"

"Each competitor receives a trinket, but I was thinking . . ." I could be sly too. "If you lose, you could give me a kiss."

Her eyes widened but not with dismay. "And what happens if I win?"

"I give *you* a kiss."

CHAPTER SEVENTEEN

KALEI

With kisses as the prize, I was going to win no matter whose bungafleer came in first place. Never in my wildest dreams did I think he'd suggest something like this. Sure, things got out of hand between us, and we took things farther than we probably should've considering we'd only recently met, but if he wanted more . . .

Yay for kisses with Forje.

I had to play this right. If—actually, *when* we kissed—I had to make sure it was good, so he'd want another. And another after that. When I'd kissed guys in the past, it hadn't worked out. One said I had too much spit—totally mortifying right there. Another said I didn't infuse my lips with enough passion. How in the universe did a girl do something like that? I didn't even want to remember what the third guy said. Something about tongues and how mine wasn't smooth enough. I'd actually contemplated taking a file to it before I realized it would be easier to ditch the guy than suffer through tongue-filing.

As for Rich, he hadn't commented. I guess him wanting

me in his bed meant my kisses were okay. Actually, though, he'd said that because he wanted easy sex.

Forje hadn't seemed displeased the other day unless . . . was that why he'd run from my room? Damn, maybe I *was* a horrible kisser.

My shoulders slumped with dismay. But then I remembered how he'd stuck his tongue in my passage and how much pleasure he gave me. A guy wouldn't do that if the woman was a crappy kisser, would he?

Probably not.

Time to switch myself into bold-Kalei mode.

"I agree to your bargain," I said.

"I am glad," he said, a heady gleam in his eyes.

Maybe he liked me and wanted to be with me tonight. He didn't appear nervous or concerned that he wasn't meeting and wooing every female in the place. He wasn't asking me to help him craft a conversation to use on someone else. He didn't seem interested in trying out Haehron dances.

My heart kept suggesting that he was spending time with me because he wanted to. Oh, my, how wonderful! If it was true . . . *Okay. Don't let down your guard fully. Watch and wait.* If he likes me, he'd show it.

I wasn't sure what to do now, so I'd take my cue from him.

With a heady grin, I glanced around before lowering my voice. "But we can't give out kiss prizes here."

"I will . . ." He frowned. "What is the term humans use? I will give you a rash check."

Rash . . .?

"You mean *rain check*." I snickered. "Sure, give me a rain check for all my hard-won kisses."

"You may be the kisser in this, lovely human, not me."

My heart flipped at the compliment. "You mean you won't kiss me back?"

He growled and leaned close to whisper in my ear. "Try me."

If only I could right now.

He waved for us to proceed, and we walked over to a table empty of other competitors.

"How do we play this game?" I took in the blocks stacked one on top of another, rising to well over Forje's very tall height.

"If your robot reaches the top of the pile before mine, you win," he said.

"Sounds easy," I said, looking for the trick. A smooth open area stretched between us and the block piles.

Forje just smiled.

Oh-kay.

I turned back to the table and sat my little skinny robot guy on the side with his legs dangling into the sunken table surface.

Forje stood his near mine.

"Is yours going to swan dive into the middle?" I asked with a smirk. I was having fun already, solely because I was hanging out with Forje.

"Are you ready?" A tall, slender alien with segmented golden skin asked. He stood on the opposite side of the table, dressed in a bright pink suit, the standard uniform for the soiree. "I am Vuleen. I will observe the event and decide who is the winner."

"I thought the robot who made it to the top first wins," I said.

"Of course, but the events go smoother if someone uninvolved makes the final judgment."

"All right." I looked up at Forje. "Will my robot know what to do?"

"Each is programmed to respond to the event it is placed in," Vuleen said.

"All right, then. On three?" I asked.

Vuleen dipped his head forward, the silver spikes jutting across the top of his head sparkling in the lights. "If you wish."

I flicked the switch on the back of my robot, and its eyes glowed bright red. Cute.

Forje's robot's eyes were pale blue but just as bright.

The two beings looked at each other and snarled.

Cool.

"Will they fight?" I asked, unsure if I wanted them to do so or not.

Forje winked at me. "Not in this event."

"Three, two, one," I said fast, then nudged my robot onto the field. He hopped down and started leaping across the open area, using his nice long legs to outdistance Forje's stockier guy with shorter legs.

Things were going well until a section of the table dropped down in front of my robot.

He tumbled into the hole and disappeared.

Forje's dude leapt across the expanse and leisurely climbed the box tower to the top, where he lifted his arms over his head and cheeped.

Huh. I trotted around to the side of the table and peered into the gap, spying my robot jumping to grab the edge but missing every time.

I scooped him up, and he went still in my hands.

"The winner of this event is Forje," Vuleen said benignly, handing him a small token that looked like a keychain but couldn't be, because no one needed them.

"It looks like you owe me a kiss," Forje whispered in my ear.

"Shall we see if we can even it up?" I asked, gesturing to another event with no competitors.

"Only if one win won't cancel the other out."

My heart flipped. Okay, so maybe I was a decent enough kisser he wanted to try again.

"Deal," I said, my voice shaky. Butlierflees danced around in my belly, and my pulse thrummed in my throat.

Vuleen strolled over to the next game with us, taking his place at the head of the table.

I studied the course made up of tiny flat stones strewn across a big pool of gook.

When I started to poke the glassy surface, Forje grabbed my hand.

"I wouldn't touch if I were you," he said.

"Why not?"

"Because it's quicksilver gloop."

"What will it do, suck me down?"

"Perhaps." His gleaming eyes hinted there might be places on me he'd like to suck. I had to be imagining this. He wasn't as hot for me as I was for him, was he?

Maybe later, I'd have a chance to find out. After all, I did owe him a kiss, didn't I?

I placed my robot on the edge of the table, and Forje did the same.

"What's the goal?" I asked.

"To reach the opposite side."

"It looks too simple." None of the rocks were far from another. A few easy hops.

"It is deceptive," Vuleen said. "Only one robot will win. There are traps your robot must avoid."

"All right." I smiled up at Forje. "On three?"

"Three," he said.

"Two."

"And . . . one."

We released our robots, who hopped off the outer rim of the table and onto the flat stones floating in the gook.

"My guy has longer legs," I said. "This will help him win this round."

"And mine has more stealth," Forje said, pointing to where his robot paused on each rock and scanned those around it. "Watch . . ."

My robot leapt from one to the next and was quickly ahead, but I had a feeling Forje was right. There was a trick here, and my robot was about to find out again what happened when someone got too bold.

The analogy wasn't lost on me. Would I lose out if I acted too boldly with Forje? I hoped I didn't find out.

A squeak rang out, and I dragged my gaze from my robot, gulping when Forje's slipped on a rock and plopped chest-first onto the gloop.

"Swim," Forje hissed. "Do not—"

His robot lowered his legs into the gloop and with a gulp, it sucked him down.

"Oh," I gulped. "It looks like . . ." I grinned as my robot hopped the rest of the way across the playing field and up onto the other side. It lifted its arms and shook its tiny hips in victory. "We won. We won!" I leaned into Forje's side, looking up at him. "I'd say we're even."

Vuleen handed me a token like Forje's and strolled to another table. I cupped it in my hand. It was nice to receive a prize, but . . .

Forje whispered in my ear. "Would you like to exchange our wins now or—"

"Forje?" someone called from the hallway beyond the bungafleer room. "Where are you?"

We both turned as a tall Haehron female dressed in a beautiful burgundy gown strode confidently across the room to join us.

She linked her arm through Forje's and blinked up at him. "Where have you been? I wanted to dance, but I could not find you."

"I . . ." His gaze met mine, and he winced. A hollowness had filled his gaze, making me wonder who she was. "Allow me to make introductions."

Yesterday afternoon, we'd practiced introducing people to each other. Now he'd use the skill to introduce me to a Haehron who was obviously crushing on him. Ugh.

"Shardeene Thorgrillidar?" he said, looking at her. "Allow me to introduce you to Kalei Bridget Sutherland. Kalei? This is Shardeene."

She nodded my way, but her gaze was solely for Forje.

Irritation mixed with worry churned through me.

"Forje and I have known each other since we were yarlings living on our home planet," she said.

"Yes," he said dully. "Since we were yarlings."

"It is time for our dance," she said firmly, leading him toward the archway leading to the ballroom.

"Perhaps later?" he said.

I had to hand it to him, he extracted himself fairly easily from her grip. He spoke with her softly before turning back to me.

She scowled and shot a glare my way before storming off across the room alone.

He returned to my side.

"If you want to go with her, you should," I said, my

happy mood gone. "You're here to find a mate, and it appears she's single."

"I am not interested in mating with Shardeene."

Shardeene had paused in the doorway to watch us.

"She looks interested in you."

"I have not seen her for a yaro. She and her family settled in a different colony."

And now they'd met up again. Had they been childhood sweethearts?

Doubts crowded in, telling me I wasn't worthy of Forje or of love, and that was just wrong. I needed to stop doing this to myself. If I pushed him away, he'd never realize I was falling for him.

Shardeene shook her head and left the room.

"What would you like to do next?" I asked brightly, hoping to restore the mood we'd slid into before Shardeene reminded me of why Forje was here. "More games?"

"If you want. Or we could get drinks and go out onto the balcony to enjoy the view."

I frowned. "Balcony? We're in the middle of space."

"You didn't know the space station has gardens?"

"No," I breathed, excitement sparking through my blood again. Pretending a boldness I didn't feel, I linked my arm through his like Shardeene had done. I even looked up at him and batted the eyelashes Callaloo had enhanced. "Would you show me?"

He grinned, the flash of his fangs making my bones melt. "Of course. I believe we owe each other kisses."

FORJE

I thought I'd lost Kalei when Shardeene appeared. I'd spoken with her earlier, before Kalei arrived, but other than catching her up on what my aunties were doing and her telling me the same about her own family, I hadn't had much to say to her.

This surprised me. I was devastated when she rejected me.

I was surprised she'd sought me out in the gaming room. We hadn't agreed to dance, so I couldn't see her purpose other than to irritate Kalei, something that made no sense.

She rejected me, not the other way around.

With a shrug, I dismissed her from my mind.

"Let us get drinks to take to the balcony with us," I said, leading Kalei into the main ballroom.

When we'd practiced social niceties back at the colony, I was nervous, unsure how I'd handle any given situation. I knew someone would say something, and I'd have no ready reply. Or that they would believe I was odd, which I was.

But with Kalei, I felt relaxed, partly because she was my

teacher and she accepted me as I was, but mostly because I enjoyed being with her.

I led her up to the bar.

"What would you like?" the male behind the counter asked Kalei.

"Do you have coosair wine?" She crinkled her nose at me. "I like the sparkles. They make me laugh."

"I will have the same," I said, needing more laughter in my life.

With our drinks in hand, I urged her through the crowd to the double doors on the opposite side of the room.

The human female who'd entered with Kalei stood beside them, watching everyone with an intent gaze.

"How are things going so far, Charlie?" Kalei asked, pausing to smile at the other female.

"Awesome," Charlie said, giving me a nod.

"I am Forje," I said.

"Nice to meet you. I'm Charlie, the head of security for the event."

"She shared my entrance so I wouldn't feel as nervous," Kalei said.

I hadn't realized she'd be worried about her arrival, and I should have. She didn't know anyone here but me and having to stand at the top of the stairs while she was announced must've played havoc with her nerves.

"Thank you," I told Charlie, warming to the woman who'd helped Kalei.

She nodded again, but frowned, staring past my shoulder. "If you'll excuse me, it appears someone has had a little too much to drink and needs to be escorted to the door."

I didn't see anyone misbehaving, but the crowd was thick, and I couldn't see everyone.

"Have a nice night," Charlie said, hurrying away.

I opened the right door and gestured for Kalei to pass through ahead of me. I was grateful she'd shown me many ways to behave in a polite manner. No wonder I blundered around during the last event I attended; I hadn't learned what was appropriate and what wasn't. My aunties tried, but their teachings didn't sink in the way Kalei's did, which was probably why they hired someone independent.

After stepping out beside her, I tugged the door shut, reducing the swell of the music that was so loud inside, it was a challenge to be heard without shouting.

"Wow, look at that," Kalei said, hurrying across the open area to stand at the rail.

"I understand they modeled this after castle balconies on Earth," I said as Kalei took in the clear arched roof that curved down some distance in front of us. Below, they'd planted gardens and set up benches and statues.

"It's amazing." She pointed toward the dome. "Look, a falling star."

"It's probably just a satellite passing the station."

She frowned, but her smile shone through. "Satellites are boring. Can't we call it a shooting star?"

I pointed to another satellite. "Look, another shooting star."

Laughing, she leaned against me, sipping her drink while pointing to particularly bright stars and even the moons on a nearby planet.

"It's quiet here," she said. "Some say there's no noise in space, but I'm not sure that's right."

"Wormholes make an eerie sound."

"Yup, it's spooky, like ghosts in a haunted house."

"I've read Earthling legends about ghosts and witches," I said. "But we don't have anything like them in our culture."

"What do you believe happens when you die?" Turning, she leaned her back against the rail and watched me, sipping her coosair.

"That is it. We die, and we cease to exist." After swallowing deeply, I recited something I'd written in the past. "We are alone like the stars, winking brightly until we are not."

"That's so sad." A shiver ripped through her. "Your people don't believe there's anything for your soul after that?"

"Like what?"

"Being with the one you love." She said it so softly, I barely heard her, but her words made me think.

I'd always believed I'd live, and then I no longer would. But what would it be like to have more than one lifetime with Kalei?

CHAPTER NINETEEN

KALEI

We watched more shooting stars that I refused to call satellites until long after we'd finished our drinks. I didn't suggest we go inside. I liked being with Forje, and he seemed to feel the same way.

Eventually, the day caught up to me, and I couldn't stop yawning.

"I bore you," he said with just a hint of dismay.

"It's not you. I'm just tired."

He took my empty glass from my hands and held out his arm. "Then I will escort you to your room."

We went inside, finding only about half the group remaining.

"Are you sure you don't want to dance?" I asked, hating that I'd kept him away from the soiree.

"Such as the waltz?" His eyes twinkled with humor. "You look tired. I think I would have to carry you around while swaying to the music."

As sweet as it sounded to be held by him, I wasn't sure I wanted to put on a performance.

"Maybe tomorrow night?" I asked.

"Tomorrow."

He led me through the narrow hallways of the space station, eventually arriving at my door. If it wasn't numbered, I would never have found it.

"Would you have breakfast with me?" he asked. "We could visit the market and dine there."

"A market?" That piqued my interest. "Sure."

His fangs flashed in a sexy smile, and he named a time.

I agreed and opened the door, stepping inside.

A sound down the hall caught my attention, and I leaned out to look, but didn't see anything.

"Thank you for tonight," I said, shrugging off the odd feeling I was being watched.

"You are welcome." Forje dipped forward in a bow before turning and striding down the hall.

That's when I realized we hadn't paid for our game losses with kisses. Should I call him back?

That might come out a bit more needy than I wanted.

I shut and locked the door, then leaned against it, mourning the loss of those kisses. It was silly, really. We shouldn't have made the bets.

He needed to start paying attention to the other females, but I'd been unable to nudge him away.

Would I be able to do so tomorrow?

CHAPTER TWENTY

FORJE

When I arrived at Kalei's door the next morning, her shriek erupted from inside.

I scrambled for a weapon, cursing that she and my aunties had talked me out of bringing my sword. At least I had a few blades sheathed at my waist.

I pulled one and kicked in the door. It blasted open, and I stormed inside, blades lifted to gouge out the throat of whoever was harming my mate.

Kalei stood on the bed, completely naked.

I quickly shut the door, though it would need work before it would lock again.

She gaped at me. "What . . .?" With a shake of her head, she pointed to the floor opposite the entrance. "Kill it. Kill it!"

Finally, a worthy challenge of my warrior skills. I rushed around the bed, prepared to impale a villain, only to find a small insect sitting on the metal flooring.

"Where is the attacker?" I asked, peering around. It was all I could do to focus. Kalei was naked. Gorgeous. More desirable than I'd ever imagined.

My cock told me it was time to rip off my clothing and claim her.

"Kill it," she shrieked again. Leaping off the bed, she raced to the door and leaned against it. "Kill it before it gets away."

"Kill what?" My mind must be scattered by her deliciousness because I'd yet to find a foe within her quarters. The cleansing room? I stormed into the tiny space and peered around, still not finding anyone to challenge.

I lowered my blades but kept a tight grip on the hilts.

"Kill the bug!" she said.

Bug . . . Returning to her bedroom, I blinked at her a minue. "You wish me to stab a small insect?"

"It crawled on me."

"How about . . ." I sheathed my blades and went around the side of her bed.

She leaped across the room and up onto the surface, comically putting herself at my eye level. I truly was much larger than her, something I needed to remember when I thought about shoving my cock inside her.

"Please kill it?" she whimpered.

"I will do even better." I scooped it up and carefully carried it out into the hall, leaving it there before returning to her. "Insects have a place in life, even on a space station. That one consumes many fleetzers, which bite and sting. It is a good insect, not one we should harm."

"It'll come back inside my room and crawl on me," she said with a shiver. Her arms went around her waist, and her lower lip trembled.

I did all I could not to gape at her lovely naked form. Staring would be impolite. Indelicate. Needy.

"I will make sure there are no others inside," I said,

keeping my gaze everywhere but on her. "Would that reassure you?"

"Yes. Thank you."

From the corner of my eye, I saw her deflate, though she remained stiffly standing on the bed. I searched the room and cleansing area quickly, returning to stand at the end of her bed, my attention on the mattress, not her lovely, awe-inspiring form.

Like lady slisps,
she is beauty in all its forms.
Lush. Exquisite. Flawless in my eyes.

A quick call on my com assured me they would send someone to fix her lock while we were gone.

As soon as I ended the call, she launched herself into my arms. I caught her. Did she know I'd always be here for her even if she shoved me away?

Did she notice she still wore no clothing? *I* did. If I offered her a covering, she might feel embarrassed. If I did not, she might think . . . I wasn't sure what she would think of that.

Shivers shook her frame, and thoughts of coverings flew from my mind. She needed me, and I was here for her. I sat on the edge of the bed, holding her until she stopped trembling.

She looked up at me, her lips quivering. "I'm sorry. I really hate bugs."

"Never apologize for being afraid." Most insects were tiny things. How could they generate hate? But if she said she hated them, I would do all within my power to keep them away from her.

"I doubt you're afraid of anything." With her face pressed against my chest, her words came out muffled.

"I fear many things."

"Like what?"

Losing her before I had the chance to be with her, though I didn't necessarily mean sex. That would give me endless pleasure, but I wanted to build something between us that would last many lifetimes. Naming it could scare her away, however, so I held in the words.

"When you run into battle, fear heightens your senses, so I give it nearly complete rein."

"That sounds healthy, actually."

"I do not allow it full control, because then my reactions will slow. But with me controlling it, I am stronger and faster. This is how I survive when others have not."

"I can't imagine doing anything like that. I don't know how to use weapons, and I'm not strong."

"Strength is an unbreakable bond within," I said softly, speaking the words from my heart. "If you hold on tight, it will never fail you."

"Is that something you read?"

"They are my words."

"They're beautiful," she whispered.

"Thank you. Someday..."

Her head tilted, and she watched my face as if she truly wished to hear what I stopped myself from saying.

I liked that her voice was starting to calm. Perhaps now was the time to offer a covering. Being honest with myself, I admitted I had no wish to cover her. I liked the feel of her body pressed against mine with very little in between.

Shaking my head, I finished my first thought. "Someday, I would like to share more of the words I have strung together."

"I think you've spoken some poetry to me in the past. Are those words yours too?"

They could be hers if she wanted them. I'd give them to her freely.

"They are. All of them." I cringed, remembering the time I'd recited a long verse to Shardeene. She'd nodded, and I thought she understood. Then, she laughed, telling me she never would. "My poems are not very good."

"The one you shared with me made my heart ache."

I sucked in a breath. "No. I rarely share them because people do not understand."

She smiled. "Like this one? We are alone like the stars, winking brightly until we are not. It's beautiful. Haunting, actually, but it spoke to me. You should never be ashamed of putting emotions to the words in your heart."

"You remembered." It humbled me and made my chest tighten.

"I'm going to remember everything you say to me, Forje."

Her words made my chest hurt even more. I tilted her face, waiting for her to pull away or change the subject, but she just stared up at me, her gaze limpid.

Did I dare?

As a warrior, I would storm across enemy lines without a thought. I'd put myself between a foe and a friend.

I didn't want to storm Kalei or push her, but . . .

Turning, I laid her on the bed, allowing my gaze to glide down her gorgeous frame.

"Beauty of the rarest find." My voice came out husky.

I composed for her alone—for my emotions alone, speaking the words in my hearts as she'd suggested.

Would she be able to tell I was falling in love with her?

"See?" she said softly. "That's beautiful."

"A gift to cherish and a prize to crave."

"Forje," she whispered, her eyes tearing. "You're going

to make me sob."

"All I want to do is give you joy." I resisted calling her mate. Not yet. Not until I was sure she felt the same as me. I couldn't bear to lose her—to have her reject me.

"You already give me joy in so many ways."

I didn't need anything more than that. Bracing myself over her, I succumbed to my feelings. I kissed her, nudging my tongue between her lips to tease across hers.

She moaned and clung to my shoulders.

As I kissed down the slender column of her neck, I nudged her legs apart with my knee.

My cock strained upward, eager, but again, it would wait. She was vulnerable so soon from her fear, and I would not do anything that might unsettle her. But that didn't mean I couldn't give her pleasure.

A glance at the door told me it held shut. Good. Now I could focus on her.

I kissed one breast, then the other. From the minue I saw them last night, I'd been eager to suck on the ripe buds, to stroke the plump mounds. When I ran my tongue across her nipple, she pulled in a breath. Her fingers bit into my shoulders, keeping me close, before sliding up to latch onto my horns.

Yes, mate. Hold me close while I make you fall apart in my arms.

I stroked down her slit with the thick head of my tail. Too often, I used my tail as a weapon. Now, it would give my mate satisfaction.

Tilting my head back, I watched pleasure fill her face as I glided my tail through her wet folds, seeking her clit.

"Yes," she whispered, rubbing her hands up and down my horns. "I want this, Forje."

"And this?" I dipped the blunted head of my tail into her

opening.

She jerked her hips up, forcing it deeper. Her guttural cry echoed around us, sending a thrill of desire up my spine. It was all I could do not to unfasten my pants, release my cock, and press it inside her.

Soon—the word was nearly a prayer. *Soon, mate.*

She thrust up to meet my tail each time I pushed it inside her.

I stroked her nipple with my tongue, coiling the thick mass around one before tugging it into my mouth. My fangs were sharp enough to rip out an attacker's throat, but they could also be gentle. I rolled the nipple between them, and her tender bud tightened.

As I moved my tail faster within her, thrusting it harder, her hoarse calls urged me on.

She bucked beneath me, rising to catch her bliss, and I tipped my head back, still rolling her nipple, watching her joy unfold on her face. There was nothing prettier or more satisfying than giving this to my mate.

Her body quivered, and I moved my tail faster, pushing in hard and pulling it back out.

Her breath caught, and she groaned, spasming around my tail while I rocked it against her.

Giving is a wondrous thing.
It fills the soul and spills outward like a rainbow,
lighting up everything in its path.
If only I could fill her world with rainbows.

When her body stopped shaking, I slowed the pace of my tail, keeping it within her, watching her come back down to the station to rejoin me.

"Forje," she gasped, stroking the tips of my horns with her thumbs. "Oh, Forje, what am I going to do with you?"

Love me, I hoped.

CHAPTER TWENTY-ONE

KALEI

What we'd just done . . . I wasn't sure how to describe it other than pure bliss. I'd do it again in a flash.

I didn't know why I'd nestled in his arms completely naked without feeling embarrassed or uncomfortable.

Well, I knew. I'd wanted to be there.

However, he must want to do more together. His poor cock strained against his pants; a big, thick thing I was curious to see and touch. I wasn't even sure if we were sexually compatible, but I was willing to try.

He eased away, falling onto my bed on his back. "That was the most amazing thing in my life."

Should I mention his cock that still shoved against his pants like a tent pole? As far as I was concerned, I'd gladly go all the way with him, but he seemed to be holding himself back.

I hated to think he did so because he expected to mate with someone else soon. It wouldn't be me; it *couldn't* be me.

When he found and claimed her, I'd hold my head high.

I'd smile and welcome her, telling her how lucky she was to have him in her life.

Nope, I had a few days at most before he could no longer be a part of my life.

So, what to do? First, use the cleansing unit and get dressed. Then go with him to the market.

And each chance I got; I'd fight for the guy I wanted.

It didn't take long to get ready, and as we walked down the hallway, aiming for what I believed was the center of the enormous structure, I held his hand. It was easy to pretend I did it to keep us from being parted. There were a lot of people about, jostling us as we passed through one intersection after another and crowding us inside the lift.

But I mostly did it because I didn't want to lose the connection we'd established between us back in my room.

"What level is the market on?" I asked inside the lift.

A dusky blue lizard stood to my right, and at my words, he turned and stared down at me, his gaze drifting from my face to Forje's before focusing on our clasped hands. I tried not to stare at his suction cup-covered limbs and big claws. He reached up and scratched his cheek, and flakes of blue scales drifted down to the floor.

I stepped backward.

"If wishessss to try messs, lets know," he said to me, his very thin and exceptionally long tongue snapping out so far it almost hit my face.

I cringed.

A low growl ripped through Forje's chest, and he pulled me fully against him, encircling me with his arms.

"No trysss, then," the lizard said with a huff, turning to face forward again.

That's when I remembered Forje telling me not to

wander around on the space station alone. If he wasn't with me, would the lizardman have asked or just taken?

A quiver shot through me at the thought of how vulnerable a tiny female was here. Much like on Earth, things never changed. Women were only sometimes given a choice.

The lift doors opened, and we made our way to the front, stepping out into the top level of the space station. Thankfully, the lizard guy remained in the car.

"Who was that?" I asked in a whisper as we took a hall to our right.

"He is a Vessar. Part of the lizard mafia. They run a prison on the planet with the two moons we saw outside the dome last night."

My spine shook. Lizard mafia? Prison?

I shook my head, scattering my fear. Forje was with me; he wouldn't let anyone harm me.

We entered a large room full of sunshine, and it melted away my lingering unease. Clear overhead panels let in the light, and a profusion of long gardens lay spread out ahead behind fences that pulsed with lasers to keep thieves from stealing the crops.

On Earth, the sun rotated around us, and each part of the planet saw day and night. The space station could control daylight by shifting behind any of the nearby planets or choosing to expose it to the sun's continual glow far in the distance. From what I'd read, they orbited in a way that created day and night like on Earth. People needed that. No one wanted to live with or without light all the time.

"This way," Forje said, leading me to the right.

We passed long rows of crops, and awe overwhelmed me. "I assumed they imported everything they needed."

"The space station is nearly self-sufficient. They grow all their crops and fabricate what they need. Even energy comes from the sun and solar wind."

"There aren't animals here for meat, I bet."

He grinned. "You'd be surprised what you'll find on the lower levels. Animal meat as a protein source is not only scarce but very expensive. Most, like at the colony where I live, we either hunt or fabricate meat products from vegetable and grain proteins. I didn't take you there, but we have vast gardens at the colony. We either donate time or credits to help maintain them."

"I'd like to see them someday." It was a silly thing to say. Although, once Forje chose a mate, my services would no longer be needed. Maybe I'd decide to remain at the colony. There must be work there for me even if it wasn't something I'd done before. I could pull weeds as well as anyone else.

Then I'd see him with his new mate. That thought stilled my heart. They'd have yarlings ...

It was too easy to picture myself holding Forje's child, a beautiful mix of us both.

My dream of a new life at the colony would die slowly, ripped apart by watching Forje move on with his life with someone other than me.

I was in love with him. I'd been attracted to him from the start, but I think I finally fell when he didn't kill the bug but put it outside my room to keep it safe. Then he held me until I stopped shivering. What happened in my bed after was wonderful too, partly because he didn't take advantage of me by pushing for full sex.

Why had I fallen for someone who'd end up with someone else?

We left the garden pavilion and entered another open

area, this one with a high ceiling draped in colorful material to provide shade. Stands had been set up in long rows, and those selling goods called out to passersby, urging them to take a look at their dried marmaly, or take a pinch of a particular spice.

I sucked in a deep breath and released it, a grin filling my face. I was sad about Forje, but the open market provided a decent distraction.

"It smells like millions of worlds combined," I said. On our right, I spied stands selling fabricated clothing. Another offered jewelry. I had a feeling I could buy almost anything I might ever want or need here.

The room pulsed with excitement, and the murmur of voices speaking a galaxy's worth of languages rippled through the air like a living beast.

"Breakfast," Forje said, rubbing his hands together. "My belly's a crater and at this rate, it's going to eat through my backbone if I don't feed it."

Mine rumbled in harmony.

"Sweet, spicy, or savory?" he asked.

"How about all of the above?"

"Now there's a female after my hearts."

I was after his hearts. Sadly, I didn't think they'd be mine.

CHAPTER TWENTY-TWO

FORJE

We found a place and ate, then wandered through the market. I didn't need to buy anything, but I savored watching the wonder on Kalei's face as she took in one item for sale after another.

"Look at those," she exclaimed, pointing to a row of animated birds. Smaller than my fist, they perched on a wire, chirping in harmony.

"I'll buy you one," I said. I'd made the offer many times.

Each time, she turned me down. "Oh, no, I can't let you do that."

"I insist. Which would you like, the blue one?"

"Well, I . . ."

I could tell she wanted one, so I urged her forward. "Take the green one, then."

The proprietor beamed, his gaze flicking between us. "They are unique in their own way and can be programmed to repeat any birdsong in the universe."

"Really?" she said in awe. "How about a chickadee? It's a common bird on Earth but one I miss most."

He nodded, flashing a smile with both sets of lips. "I can do cheek-a-dee."

She glanced up at me. "All right. Thanks." When she pointed at the black and white bird, the clerk programmed it. Strangely enough, the bird spoke its name, cheek-a-dee. He handed it to her, taking the necessary credits with a scan of my wrist com.

"Thank you," she said, holding the bird against her chest. Her heart was there, and I wanted it.

Could I win her for always?

"You are welcome," I said gruffly.

We wandered some more, her speaking to the bird who kept repeating its name. Each time, she laughed.

I loved pleasing her and wanted to do so again. So, when we stopped to gaze at the wares on display at a jeweler's stand, I offered to buy her something else.

"No, I love my bird," she said, running a finger down its back feathers. "That's enough."

"What about this one?" I wasn't ignoring her wishes. I could tell by the wonder in her eyes that she'd like something from the shop. It made me realize I should ensure she was paid soon—and generously. I didn't like her scrimping to survive.

I held up a chain with a small pendant set with a prillar stone.

"It's pretty." She touched the pendant with the tip of her finger, and it spun, generating flashes of blue light.

"We will take it," I told the proprietor as I secured the fastening at the back of her neck. I was more than tempted to kiss her nape. We'd been intimate a few times, but I still didn't know where we stood. Did she believe I sought a mate through the Match-Mating Soiree? What if I asked her to be my mate, and she told me she wasn't interested in anything permanent?

No, I would continue to wallow in my dreams of us being together, hoping to find a way to make my dream come true.

She stroked the pendant as we continued through the market, but eventually, we had to leave to get ready for the evening's festivities.

I escorted her back to her room and was grateful the lock was fixed and Callaloo had arrived to help Kalei get ready. I left her in Callaloo's capable hands and went to my own quarters to prepare.

Fear of rejection be damned.

Tonight was the night I'd tell Kalei I wanted *her* for my mate.

CHAPTER TWENTY-THREE

KALEI

This time, when I stepped into the ballroom and they announced me, Forje was waiting on the top step. Had he been here most of the time I was getting ready?

He stretched out his hand. "Would you like to dance?" On cue, music for a waltz drifted through the air. A few aliens standing nearby frowned, and those remaining on the dance floor after the last dance glanced at each other.

What a time to lead.

But I did want to dance with Forje, so I took his hand. "Thank you."

"I believe I understand how to do this," he said, guiding me to the middle of the floor.

In no time, I was soaring around the nearly empty room in his arms, and there was nothing I'd rather do than that. Well, except be alone with him.

Others cautiously joined us, some swaying while a few picked up the steps from us and were soon performing as if they'd done the waltz all their lives. Perhaps they'd learned it elsewhere?

We ended up dancing three waltzes before retreating

off the dance floor. It looked like the waltz had taken over, as the floor was filled with dancers, and I sensed the music wouldn't stop soon.

"Shall we retreat to the balcony?" he said with a laugh.

At my nod, he led me in that direction. We stopped beside Charlie, who stood near the door again, watching the room.

"No concerns?" Forje asked, his fingers tapping the hilt of the blade he wore on his side. Ever the military guy ready to defend us.

Frankly, it made me feel safer after my encounter with the lizardman in the lift.

"Yes," Charlie said. "Earlier, we were concerned about . . ." She stiffened and dragged her gaze away from us. "About nothing."

"What were you concerned about?" Forje pressed.

She shook her head. "I told you. Nothing."

"All right." With a curt nod, Forje guided me out onto the balcony.

We weren't there long before we heard someone inside calling his name.

Shardeene?

"Well," he said, his gaze meeting mine, "should we let her know where we are or should we . . . avoid her?"

"What do you want to do?" I asked hesitantly. Despite what he'd said the night before, he may want to dance with her.

"We could run away before she finds us."

I chuckled at his sparkling eyes, enjoying being part of the game he played. "That would be undignified, wouldn't it?"

He shrugged. "We run, or we wait here for her to arrive."

No thanks.

I snickered. "Let's scoot down there?" I pointed to a set of stairs leading downward. "We can take a walk in the garden and discuss the prizes we forgot to give each other after the game last night."

How could I forget?

I was never one to pass up the chance of kissing Forje.

"You are right. You owe me a kiss."

"And you owe me one." My blood thrilled through me, sparking both desire and excitement as we hurried down the stairs.

CHAPTER TWENTY-FOUR

FORJE

As we reached the bottom of the stairs, she smiled. It sunk into my bones; a caress I'd seek for the rest of my dias.

Warm, sultry air greeted us in the gardens.

"It's beautiful here," she said, pointing to the two moons rising above one of the large, nearby planets. Light sparkled on the real grass at our feet and highlighted the numerous flowerbeds. "I can't believe there's this enormous garden on the space station covered with a clear dome."

"The space station is amazing."

"I wonder if you should consider building a dome like this at the colony. I know it would take a lot of materials, but it would protect your crops from predators and whoever else might attack."

"Like the Twarvians."

She stopped at a bench and sat, patting the space next to her, which I took. "I've heard about the Twarvians. They used to be endangered, but I think I read they no longer are?"

"They are not. The few they found on a space station were brought to the planet me and my family now call home. They were given their own territory, but they are carnivores, and we are their most sought-after prey. Despite the wall we built around our colony as protection, they try to scale it to eat us."

Her body quivered, and I put an arm around her shoulders. I doubted she was cold; she was scared like so many of my fellow colonists.

"It is my job to protect everyone in the colony. No Twarvian will get past me and my squadron."

"Can you do that for the rest of your life?"

She spoke the words my aunties often said when I returned from a battle.

Should I tell Kalei? I'd tried with Shardeene, but she brushed my ideas away, saying they weren't anything that interested her.

Actually, I needed to tell Kalei. I wanted her in my life if she'd have me; I had almost from the moment I met her. She should know my plans. Perhaps she hoped to fit in with them.

"I plan to resign from the military soon, but I want to remain at the colony as a regular resident."

Her breath caught. "What will you do?"

"Would it sound strange if I said I want to farm? I've always enjoyed working with creatures and planting crops. Your idea for a dome is perfect, and I can see incorporating it into the colony. Perhaps covering the entire area to permanently keep the Twarvians out if another solution isn't found soon."

"Maybe it would be easier to cover them with a dome," she said in a low voice.

"We would need interstellar council permission for that."

"If they're attacking you, they're not good neighbors. I can't imagine the council, who must've approved your colony, allowing the Twarvians to keep trying to eat you."

"I will bring it up with them again."

"Again?" she asked, leaning into my side and looking up at me.

"The last time I introduced the topic at a council meeting, I was told to leave things as they are. But the situation is untenable, and none of us can find a solution other than leaving the planet or building our wall higher."

"That doesn't seem fair."

It wasn't, but we were at the mercy of the council. Where would we go if we left Davoome? It was our home, now, and we enjoyed living there despite the Twarvians.

"I have planted a wellire seed for a home beyond the outskirts of the town. I have built a barn, as well. I did this during my free time." I said the last hastily, worried she'd think I ignored my position to further my future. "When I resign from the military, I will move there and plant my crops."

"What about Enzia and Rozen?"

"If they wish to come with me, they are more than welcome, though they love living in town where they can visit with friends. My wellire in the country will be large enough for them, plus . . . yarlings."

"What creatures do you want to put in your barn?" she asked.

"Animals to help me till my crops, those I can milk, and a few I can ride."

"Can you buy them locally?"

"I will track them in the woods and bring them back to tame them."

Her eyes widened. "Is that easy?"

I shrugged. "Probably not, but where else would I obtain them? I have heard of creatures one might buy from distant planets, but I am uncertain I want to introduce different species to our colony. It might be best to tame those in the area already."

"What kind of home do you plan?" she asked. Did I hear longing in her voice? Shardeene chose not to mate with a farmer. The environment on the planet, let alone the Twarvian threat, made settling in the colony a challenge.

I could better attract Kalei with my military position and income, but farming was a dream I'd had since I was young. Would I let it go if it meant I could be with Kalei?

Yes.

"I need to tell you something about Shardeene," I said. "I was preparing to ask her to be my mate, but it did not work out. We hadn't formally matefasted, so there was no . . . divorce, as you call it on Earth. We parted."

"Ah, I'd wondered if there was something between you."

"She rejected me after I shared my poetry and dreams for my future. She wanted to be mated with a military commander, not a farmer. It hurt, but now . . ."

She held her breath. "Now what?"

"Now I cannot understand why I ever wanted to mate with her."

Kalei's breath whooshed out. "Okay. I understand. It was the same with Rich. I thought I wanted to be with him, but once we were together, it was horrible. I can't imagine why I ever wanted him."

"In this, like growing up with aunts, we are alike."

"Inside, people are the same. I've always believed that. We break down to one thing, the dream of being happy. I'm sorry she hurt you."

"It was for the best." If I was with Shardeene, I never would've met Kalei, and I could not imagine not having her in my life.

She shot me a smile. "Tell me more about your farming dream."

"I've started small," I said.

"Started?"

"I've already claimed a piece of land and cleared enough of the forest for a big field. My wellire is half-grown already, and the upper rooms are beginning to form."

"I'd love to see it," she said wistfully. "I can't imagine growing a home from a seed."

"It was a big seed, half the size of my body."

"Wow."

"I could show you what they look like sometime." I watched her face. "And the start of my farm."

"I'd love to see it. Maybe when we return to the colony?"

"I will set up a time to visit," I said, my hearts soaring. "This is all I have ever wanted." Perhaps one day, I would share the new wellire with her. "It is common to move in before the wellire has finished growing, so I expect to live there when there is only one bedroom and a large meal preparation area. I will have a place to sit in the evening in front of the fire."

"It sounds really cute. Cozy. And I can't imagine building a fire inside a wellire, but how else will you generate heat?"

"The plants keep a neutral temperature inside, but they are subject to extremes like anything else. In the winter, it can get quite cold outside, so additional heat helps keep the inside of the wellire warm."

My hearts stopped battering against my ribcage and relaxed. She liked my idea. Now to convince her to share it with me.

"Will you have a cleansing unit?" she asked.

"I have no interest in stepping into the woods to take care of my needs or jumping into an icy river to get clean," I said with a laugh.

"You never know. Icy water might feel . . . invigorating."

"Would you swim in icy water?" I asked, truly curious.

"It depends on who I'm swimming with and if they're eager to warm me up."

My cock perked up in my pants, stating it was more than eager to warm Kalei.

Down, I chided it. *Behave.*

It didn't like behaving. It had a one-track mind, and it was focused on her.

"Do you see yourself with anyone at your farm? Someone would have to help you with your, um . . . yarlings," she said, tracing her finger along the bench edge on her left. She didn't look up, but her tensed shoulders told me she was listening. "I assume you still plan to mate even if it's not with someone you meet at the soiree."

"I did," I said. "I do." I gulped and threw my hearts out there at the urging of my cock. "I've picked someone I plan to ask to be my mate."

CHAPTER TWENTY-FIVE

KALEI

Oh, shit, shit, shit.

He'd picked out a mate. She could be anyone.

Jealousy I shouldn't feel filled me. Was it Shardeene? No, not her. He just said she rejected him. Surely, he wouldn't take her back after that?

He planned to have children with someone else.

Unless . . .

Was it silly to hope he meant me? I should step out and let him know how I felt about him. If I let him go without telling him I cared, I'd never know if I lost him because I hadn't put myself out as an option.

And maybe if I took a chance, I'd find myself with Forje as my mate.

My hands shook, but I stiffened my resolve.

"Have you asked this person to be your mate yet?" I asked.

"I have not."

So there was still time, and I was going to make the most of it. "Who do you see as your mate?"

"Someone special. Someone who may not know that I want her."

I wish I dared ask him who she was.

"Where should we exchange prizes?" I asked; a wild question considering he'd just told me he was going to mate with someone else. But I wanted one more kiss—or two, actually, since I'd give him one and he'd do the same.

My heart kicked into high gear, and my pulse thrummed in my ears.

Somewhere nearby, laughter rang out shrilly, reminding me a lot of people attended the soiree.

"I am in no rush," he said, waving to the gardens in general. "Would you like to walk?"

At my nod, he took my hand, and I marveled at how long his fingers were and how his palm engulfed mine. Even in heels, the top of my head didn't reach his shoulders.

We strolled down a path with tall hedges on either side. Someone had planted tuleskar flowers and their petals had opened, something that only happened when moonlight hit them. The glowing flowers released a lovely perfume.

Forje stopped and picked one. He carefully worked the stem into my hair, so the blossom nestled above my ear.

"You're lovely," he said, gliding the back of his hand across my cheek.

"Thank you. And thanks for arranging for Callaloo to help me get ready each night."

With a smile, he took my hand again, and we continued down the path that slowly curved along the back of the property. Stone benches had been placed here and there, and big urns full of siskette water glowed. I stopped and watched as the iridescent yellow and green fish darted through the small pools. As they shifted, arcs of light shot off them, spearing toward the top of the dome. I had to keep reminding myself I was still within the space station and not on a planet far from here.

At the farthest point from where we left the ballroom, we came upon a raised area with piles of cushions lining two sides. A fake fire had been lit in the center, and globule binny balls hung above the area, filled with delecta that sparkled gold, giving a nice glow to the cozy setting.

"Would you like to sit and enjoy the fire?" he asked.

With Forje? Any day of the week and on weekends too.

"Sure," I said, keeping it neutral.

We settled on the cushions side-by-side.

He gestured to the low table by our feet. "A drink of umbarla?" At my nod, he poured and handed me a glass of amber liquid, then filled another fluted glass for himself. With a clink, he tapped our glasses together. "To the Haehron colony and the endless possibilities we'll find here."

I wasn't yet sure about my possibilities there, though I suspected they were looking up.

I took a sip, savoring the fruity flavor of the umbarla that was made from the fermented fruit.

"Will others be upset that you're out here with me instead of entertaining them?" I asked.

"There's nowhere else I want to be than here with you."

"I'm having a nice time tonight too."

Turning, he fully faced me. "I want to kiss you."

Was that the umbarla talking? He'd only drank a small amount.

My heart thrilled, and I nodded.

His fingers cupped my cheeks, and he leaned close, his breath warm on my face. His mouth came down on mine, and I expected sweetness with heat. Or for him to lean back and smile.

I never dreamed I'd feel like I was bursting into flames solely from his touch.

CHAPTER TWENTY-SIX

FORJE

I couldn't believe I was holding Kalei in my arms again, and kissing her. We'd done things together that other couples do, but neither of us had spoken the words I ached to hear. That she liked me. That she wanted to be with me always.

She moaned and wiggled closer, settling on my lap with her legs spread around my waist while still maintaining our kiss.

Heat flared inside me, a raging inferno that would never be extinguished.

We burst apart, and she smiled. "You're pretty addictive, Forje."

"So are you."

For the first time, I began to believe there was a chance we'd end up together. I didn't want to lose this moment. I didn't want to lose her.

"You are sweet, and you make my hearts beat faster."

"That makes me want to cry," she said softly.

"I want you to have everything wonderful in the world."

A smile rose on her face, and it warmed me through.
"I want to kiss you again," I said.
"Then what's stopping you?"
I didn't want to take this too far.
Or did I?

CHAPTER TWENTY-SEVEN

KALEI

He laid me back on the cushions and rose over me, big and hulking, and incredibly strong.

I rubbed his arms, savoring his weight pressing down on my body.

His mouth feathered across mine, both sweet and with growing fire. It sparked something inside me I couldn't contain.

For dias, I'd only dreamed of being with this guy. This was my chance to show him how wonderful we could be together.

His fingers teased along my sides, and I wished I wasn't wearing a silly gown even if it didn't show off my boobs. I wanted to be wearing nothing.

But when he stroked across my breast, all thought fled, replaced with raw need.

I moaned, and his fingers stilled.

He started to back away. "I shouldn't be—"

I pressed my finger against his lips, savoring the plumpness. "You're not taking anything I'm not willing to give."

He stared deeply into my eyes before giving me another

kiss, this one drinking from me, drawing it out until I felt like I blended with him. It should be scary to lose all sense of myself, but getting lost in Forje felt like the most natural thing in the world.

He kissed each of my fingertips in turn before staring down at me. "How far do you wish to take this, sweetheart?"

My heart flipped at the term of endearment. On his tongue, it sounded real, not just a funny nickname used for one night.

"How far?" I asked, cocking my head like I needed to think about this before giving him an answer.

As if.

"You can take this as far as you want," I finally said.

CHAPTER TWENTY-EIGHT

FORJE

My cock, willful thing that it was, battered against my pants, determined to rip its way free.

Determined to find a way inside her.

Sweetheart. My Kalei. I began to believe I'd get to claim her.

"What if I want to do this?" I asked, bunching up her skirt until her panties peeked from the edge of the fabric.

"I'd say you should do it." She watched my face, my eyes, and her lips parted in anticipation.

"And what if I did this?" I glided my thumb down her undergarment, groaning when I found it wet between her legs.

Her hips jerked up, and her eyelids slid half-closed.

"I think I have my answer," I said.

I was obsessed with her glorious breasts. Females on my planet had four breasts, yet I found Kalei's two to be perfect. She didn't need more to attract me. And her nipples. I'd already discovered they became aroused when touched. Even through the fabric, I felt them budding.

It was all I could do to drag my gaze off her breasts last

evening as she strode across the ballroom floor. They shifted on her chest, perky and sweet, and I'd do almost anything to touch them.

She lifted her chest and moaned as I glided a finger carefully along her flesh. I circled her nipple.

Her breathing had gone ragged but so had mine. We charged toward the edge of the cliff, and nothing was going to keep us from plunging over the other side.

She was sweet and she already held my hearts. I wouldn't do anything that might hurt her.

I kept taking tastes but never the full meal. I wouldn't do that until I was confident that she truly wanted to be with me.

"How much do you enjoy this garment you're wearing beneath your dress?" I asked.

"My panties?" she asked, her voice languid and budding with need. "Not much."

"Good." With a grin, I sliced it away with the claw on my thumb.

She gasped in shock but moaned when I slid my claw through the wetness gushing from between her folds.

I kissed the mounds of her breasts, enjoying the full yet soft feel. She arched her spine and invited me to do whatever I pleased with them, and that was all I needed.

I tugged her dress down and sucked one nipple into my mouth, gliding my scratchy tongue across it. Before Kalei, I'd never been with a human female before, but I'd read about their males. Their tongues were not scratchy, and they did not have flairs on the sides of their cocks. I couldn't understand how they satisfied their mates.

My single goal tonight was to show Kalei pleasure.

CHAPTER TWENTY-NINE

KALEI

Forje crouched between my legs and spread them wide, then started licking the most intimate part of my body. And when he did that, every thought flew from my mind. All I could focus on was the scratchy stroke of his tongue and his fingers rubbing my clit.

His tongue delved inside me, long and thick. I knew right then that my instincts had been right. This guy was hot. He was made for me. And I wanted him desperately. It was time to put my ex behind me and let someone new—and infinitely better—take his place.

A groan ripped up my throat, and a wildness took over me, turning me into a feral creature. I bucked and strained, spreading my legs wider to give him access.

His hand rested on my belly, holding me down, and when he chuckled, the vibration quivered through my bones. I wanted so much. This moment to last forever. For him to truly like me for who I was. And for us to take this further than tonight.

I wanted to be his forever mate.

He licked and sucked me like I was a feast and him

starving. "You are amazing," he mumbled against my flesh. He pulled my clit into his mouth and rolled it gently between his teeth.

I bucked, my hoarse cries echoing in the small area. If he kept at it, I was going to scream, and they'd call the sergeants to investigate a probable murder.

That was me, my clit being decimated in the most delightful way by Forje.

He dragged his tongue across my clit before dipping it inside me again, driving it all the way to the end. How that was possible, I did not know, but I wasn't going to analyze it at a time like this.

Like before, I swore sparks flickered deep inside me. They didn't hurt; they only made me want him more.

I pumped my hips, my mind a blur. My sole focus was on his mouth, my engorged clit, and the way his other hand rolled my nipple.

I latched onto his horns to keep myself from tumbling over the cliff and plunging down the other side.

Riding the crests, I rocked against him, keening. I'd lost all sense of myself.

"Fall apart for me," he said before driving his tongue back inside me.

My cry burst from me as I gave way, a landslide rushing down the hill to engulf the world.

I came to rest in Forje's arms.

CHAPTER THIRTY

FORJE

There was nothing purer than giving Kalei pleasure. It made my hearts flip over.

It made my cock ache. How much longer could I resist being with her fully? I didn't want to do anything that would ruin things like I had with Shardeene. We were together, and then she rejected me.

I helped Kalei straighten her clothing and sit up, tugging her onto my lap. I didn't want to lose contact with her.

"I don't know what to say," she said, tucking her face against my chest. "Thank you."

"I want to do it again."

"You already have." She laughed, a light sound that made my pulse roar. Everything about her pulled me in. I'd willingly drown in her touch.

"Would you stay the night with me?" I asked. "In my room. My bed."

Her breath caught. "I'd like that. But . . ."

"You can say no." Frankly, there wasn't anything I'd rather see than Kalei stretched out on my bed completely naked but perhaps I was pushing this once again. I refused to mess this up like I had with Shardeene.

"You probably think I'm being silly. I want to but . . . I'm shy. You make me feel things I never had before, and it scares me."

"Tonight feels special. I worried no one would be interested in spending time with me at the soiree, but that is not the only reason I wish to be with you tonight. I want you, Kalei. You."

"I enjoy being with you." Her voice deepened. "And yes, I will stay the night with you."

I wanted to tip my head back and roar. Cover her face with kisses. My thoughts were scattered, and I couldn't grab hold of them.

I wanted to lie her back on the cushions and eat her out all over again. Make her come twice this time.

Would it be bad to skip the party and take her to my room now?

"I suppose we should be getting back," she said sadly. "The other guests must be wondering where you went."

"I do not care about them." I only cared about her.

"We could dance." She grinned up at me. "You said something about lifting me and twirling me around the room?"

I stood, still holding her in my arms. "We will dance here."

"There's no music."

"What if I hum?"

She cocked her head. "How's your singing voice?"

"Horrible, but I shall put my hearts into it."

"Then that's good enough for me."

CHAPTER THIRTY-ONE

KALEI

He danced around the meadow with me in his arms, and soon, my wild laughter rang out. I'd never dreamed I'd get this close to Forje. Now we were dancing and soon, we would go to his room and . . .

I'd let him do whatever he pleased because I planned to do the same.

He tripped over a bush and toppled onto the ground on the other side.

I landed hard on his chest with my legs straddling his thighs, and his breath whoofed out.

His laughter echoed around us as his arms went around my waist. "You are a petite little thing."

I tapped his chest. "I am not." Though I appreciated him saying it.

He ran his hands up my sides. "You are lush. Gorgeous. Incredibly sexy."

"Really?" My voice came out breathy, but he was the one who'd been twirling about.

"Really." He stroked his palms beneath my dress, along my thighs, pausing at the juncture he'd licked not long ago.

His eyelids hooded and watching the pleasure he got from touching me unfold on his face was all I needed. How had we gone from dancing to bursting into flames?

I leaned forward and kissed him, savoring how his mouth drank from mine as if he was starving, and I was the only meal he needed.

Forje's fingers moved higher and each time they reached the juncture between my thighs, he ran his thumb claw across my clit.

I was going to come from this alone but . . .

His gaze and his hands on my thighs urged me on, letting me take the lead.

I stroked down his chest while he teased my clit with his claw. A wild craving rose inside me. I'd been with my ex many times, but more often than not, he was the only one who got pleasure out of it.

With Forje, I had a feeling it was going to feel good every single time. And if it didn't, he'd make sure the next time gave me complete pleasure. My needs would be as important as his.

My fingers worked their way down his chest, undoing each button of his shirt. I paused to stroke his abs because they were amazing. I could drool over them every day of the week, and why did he keep them covered?

But my fingers stilled at the top of his pants. How far would he let me take this?

We kept playing with full sex but never going all the way.

Now was the time. I trusted him enough to give myself fully.

I looked up at him, my gaze locking with his. "If you want me to stop, now would be the time to tell me."

He groaned and shook his head, giving me permission to do whatever I pleased.

With a sly smile, I undid his pants, releasing his big, thick cock.

CHAPTER THIRTY-TWO

FORJE

"It's very large," she said, licking her lips as she stared at my cock. "And what are these lovely things along the bottom?"

"Fressar flares. They tighten and throb when I'm aroused."

"They're tightening, which I'll take as a good sign. And wow. They vibrate."

"They want you. *I* want you." My fingers were buried between her legs, and her skirts pooled around us. I couldn't get over how wet she was. I kept sliding the blunt side of my claw through her folds, making sure to include her engorged clit in my efforts.

She sucked in a breath. "You just said the magic words, Forje." Rising over me, she centered my cock at her saturated opening.

Then she dropped down, using the weight of her tiny body to push me all the way inside her sheath.

"Not too big," she said, wiggling to accept everything I had to offer. "I'd say you fit just right."

She was a wild thing. *My* wild thing. She just didn't yet know it.

My fressars flared further, turning into soft yet rigid spikes, and they started to quiver.

"Oh, wow," she said, her eyes rolling back in her head. "Those ridges . . . I'm going to come in seconds if you keep that up."

"I intend to keep it up as long as you need it," I grated out, thrusting up each time she dropped down.

My cock was aflame for her alone.

She rode me, bouncing and moaning, her head thrust back with bliss, her neck exposed to the night air. Her skirts shifted around us, and for one second, I figured I had to be dreaming. But when she moaned again and moved faster, I knew this was real. I was with Kalei, and my dreams were coming true.

I plunged up to meet her, my eyes rolling back in my head. A herd of cendairy deer could gallop past us and some could leap over us, and I wouldn't care.

"I'm gonna . . ." she keened.

"Do it." I was going to come too.

I rubbed her clit harder, and she began to shudder.

"Those ridges are amazing. They hit my G-Spot just right. I can only imagine where they'll rub if you take me from behind."

A deficit I'd need to take care of as soon as possible.

She bounced faster, her breasts jiggling each time she slammed down. All I could do was stare and keep thrusting up to meet her. Everything I'd ever wanted was within my reach. Finally, I would claim my mate and she would not leave me.

It was all I could do not to blast my cum deep inside her

this second. I had to hold off. Her pleasure was all that mattered.

She shuddered and leaned forward, her lips pressing against my chest.

I drove my hips up, pushing myself inside her over and over, savoring how her wet flesh sucked on my cock. Her passage clung to me, milked me. I'd never experienced anything like it and part of the reason why this felt so good was because I was with *her*.

I'd craved Kalei since the moment I met her, and now, she was mine.

Her spine went rigid, and her thighs tightened around my hips. "Yes, yes," she sighed. "Yes."

When she collapsed on top of me, spent, I gave way, shooting everything I had into her welcoming sheath.

We lay on the ground, breathing hard, and I couldn't stop grinning. Yes, I was male, so of course I was happy this woman had driven my cock into her body and rode me until we both came. But I was with Kalei, the only female I would ever love.

Would she let me do it again soon?

"Forje?" Shardeene called out from a few hedges over.

"Oh, my," Kalei gulped, gaping down at me. She scrambled with her skirts, yanking them down around her thighs. A smile of pure satisfaction crossed her face, and she looked down at me, licking her lips. "Well, since I'm still riding you, I'm not sure what good covering my legs will do."

Her licking her lips was all my cock needed. It kicked into high gear again, straining upward.

"Forje?" Shardeene called out again. "Where are you?"

Her footsteps hurried in our direction.

CHAPTER THIRTY-THREE
KALEI

"Forje?"

Damn Shardeene for interrupting the best moment of my life.

Forje grinned up at me and damn if his cock wasn't stiffening already. Would she notice me humping him if she passed close by?

Probably. She had an uncanny way of finding Forje whenever she wanted.

Forje helped me climb off, my body sucking on his cock as it slipped out of me. His fressar flares had tightened again and the lush vibration echoed within my bones.

I was ruined for anyone but him. No other cock would do.

I hadn't intended for anything like this to happen. The minue got away from us both. But being with him felt good. Right.

We stood, and I dragged my skirt down farther.

He winced, struggling to stuff his thick rod back into his pants and fasten them. "Get in there, you."

"You speak to your cock?"

"I do." His lips curled up on one corner. "You can do so, too, whenever you please."

I might be able to get into something like that, but not in front of Shardeene.

"Should we wait here for her to arrive?" he whispered.

What a question. I peered around, looking for a bench. We could sit and pretend we were just talking. As long as Shardeene didn't notice the overgrown vegetable filling his pants, she might believe we hadn't been doing anything else.

But why bother with her?

"I'd rather not," I said. "What other options are on the table?"

With a sexy smile, he held out his hand. "Run away again?"

My breath caught, frozen in my chest by excitement. The possibilities here were endless.

I placed my hand in his, just like I'd pretty much handed him my heart the first time I met him.

"Forje? Where are you?" Shardeene called. "Why can't I find you?"

Because I was hiding him. Monopolizing him. Keeping him away from *her*. Was it mean of me to leave her wandering around the gardens, seeking him?

Nah.

Forje must've agreed. He flashed me a grin before turning and darting in the opposite direction, me running beside him.

I held back my laughter that was so eager to spring out. It would give us away.

Our footsteps remained light as we darted along a path leading along the side of the dome.

These gardens were huge, taking up more of the space station than I'd ever imagined. But comfortable public spaces were just as important as private ones. It made sense they'd use this vital square footage for a park.

I'd read the person who designed the space station had won awards and that others were copying this design. For a while, it was all Earthlings talked about. Many wanted to move here, but immigration was limited to those with specific skillsets, at least initially. The goal was to create so many stations that whoever wanted to live on them could.

We rounded a curve in the path, and a long area covered in tall grass spread out ahead of us with a forest of mushroom trees beyond. Wellires? If so, they were much smaller than those Forje and his people lived in. These didn't have big caps that could be turned into dwellings. Perhaps these were a similar species.

Forje paused, probably unsure where to run to next.

"Forje?" Shardeene called out.

Damn, she was persistent. And she was catching up to us!

I tugged Forje up the short hill to the flat area, and we took a path weaving through the grass. We snaked along it, the grass on both sides almost as tall as Forje, and Shardeene's voice slowly faded.

Finally, we came to a stop and flopped on the ground, compressing the grass around us in a small circle.

"Do you think we lost her?" I asked, snickering.

"I believe so."

Because I felt proprietary about his body, I climbed onto his lap. His arms went around me, and I snuggled against his chest. Mmm . . . He smelled amazing, like fresh air and whatever scent setting he'd used to cleanse his laundry.

He tipped my chin up so our eyes could meet. "I'm glad we ran away together."

"Me too."

When he kissed me, a moan rumbled in my chest.

And when he laid me on the grass and rose above me, I decided it was time to give him everything all over again.

CHAPTER THIRTY-FOUR

FORJE

I'd fully intended to take Kalei to my room where I could lay her on my bed and devour her, savoring each lick and nibble. But when we kissed, all thought of soft beds and silky sheets flew out of my mind.

She dominated my every thought, from her smooth flesh to her warm mouth to the soft sighs she released that told me how much she enjoyed my touch.

And when she nudged me away, sat up, and wiggled out of her dress, tossing it aside, all I could do was groan.

"Is it bad that I'm inviting you to do whatever you want with me now instead of inside your room?" she whispered.

"Not at all." I flashed her a smile, nearly overwhelmed with excitement. This woman wanted me despite my odd poetry and dreams of being a farmer. There was nothing better than that. I hadn't ruined things by allowing her to ride me, and I sensed if *I* rode *her*, I still wouldn't destroy what we were building together. Everything I'd ever wanted was finally happening. Waiting for the right person meant nothing when the result was happiness for a lifetime.

"I suggest you take off your clothing," she said in a husky voice.

My hearts surged, and my hands shook as I removed my suit jacket. My aunties fabricated a bunch of formal clothing for me, insisting I wear them for the soiree. Since I wanted to impress Kalei, I'd agreed. I wanted to look good for her, appealing.

I wasn't the type of guy females salivated over. My awkward, gruff personality kept them away. But I figured if I could improve my outside appearance, she might notice me. Never in my wildest dreams did I believe I'd strip off this suit so I could love her.

Light strokes her face,
highlighting her pretty features,
making me crave her like no other.

"That's beautiful, Forje," she said, her eyes sparkling. Did she cry for me? I didn't want that.

"I mean the words, Kalei," I said gruffly. "Truly."

"Thank you."

By my touch and with my poem, I hoped she'd see that I'd only ever want *her*.

My cock kept pushing, demanding a way out, the unruly thing, but this minue was about more than sex. I wanted to experience the sublime moment I'd only find in Kalei's arms.

I'd love her and show her how much I wanted her. And maybe after that, she'd agree to be my forever mate.

CHAPTER THIRTY-FIVE

KALEI

I was in a fever for him. Nothing was going to stop me now. When I saw him in his suit earlier, I'd practically swooned. But the suit was only second best when compared to naked Forje.

Every bit of him rippled with muscles that must've come from battle, plus clearing his land and working his growing farm.

Would he invite me to see it one day? I could picture myself farming with him, nursing each new plant until it grew big and strong. I saw us sitting in the tiny living room he described or laying together in front of the fire. Cooking in the kitchen.

Retiring to the bedroom each night.

But I was getting ahead of myself. One thing at a time.

His abs needed my attention as well as the big cock below. Any day of the week and twice on Sundays!

"Forje?" Shardeene called from nearby. "We really need to talk. I . . . I made a mistake."

What did he want to do? I doubted he'd listen, but he'd

cared for her once. I'd step back if he needed to speak with her.

"What do you want to do?" I whispered.

"I have nothing to say to her."

I loved hearing the confidence and resolve in his voice. Grabbing my dress off the ground, I flashed him a grin. "Then let's run."

His low laugh rang out as he snatched up his clothing. He took my hand, and we bolted along a path, not stopping even when we reached the skinny mushroom forest. We wove through the woods with moonlight guiding our way, not stopping until we were out of breath and panting.

He still had a raging hard-on, and I backed against a tree, curling my finger his way.

"If you want me, come get me." I dropped my gown, and it fluttered to the forest floor.

With a heady growl, he stalked right up to me, not stopping until his naked flesh pressed me against the tree. He lifted me up so our mouths could meet, and he devoured me while his fingers glided up and down my sides.

I wrapped my legs around him, pressing against his cock. It was too low with our mouths locked together, so I released him and slid down his body, stopping only when the head of his cock met my opening.

He watched me as he ran a thumb claw across my nipple.

I sucked in a breath and wiggled, wanting to feel him driving deeply within me.

His hands were everywhere, tweaking my nipples and even reaching down between us to rub my clit.

It was wild and exciting.

"Claim me," I whispered. "Make me yours."

With a groan, he braced my hips and drove himself hard within me.

"Yes," I hissed, pressing my face against his chest.

He began moving, slowly at first, but at my urging, faster, pummeling me with his cock and his body. The tree back was smooth behind me, and the subtle rub felt amazing.

While I clung to him, he loved me with what felt like everything inside him. I remembered his poem and his vow. His words meant the world to me, as did this moment.

His fressar flares rubbed my inner passage while his hands roamed my body. He kept my nipples aching buds and my clit a throbbing wreck. I panted and whimpered, begging him for more.

Forje more than delivered, surging up into me over and over.

I was liquid. I was his. He could do whatever he wanted with me, and I'd take it and more.

"Come for me," he grated out. "I want to feel it. Feel you falling apart in my arms."

He pushed harder, delving deeper, the flares on the underside of his cock gliding across my G-spot.

My breath hitched as everything inside me gathered into a big bunch, a mass that would shoot all the way across the universe when I came undone.

"You come for me," I snarled, nipping at his chest. I sucked one of his nipples into my mouth and ran my tongue across it, savoring how his body shivered at my touch.

He lifted my chin, his other hand bracing me.

And when our gazes locked, his hand slipped between us. His fingers stroked my clit, and that was all it took.

I blazed in his arms, everything inside me coming undone. I quivered and shook while he rode me harder, drawing out all of me and scattering me across the galaxy like the words of his beautiful poems.

FORJE

I came with a heartfelt groan, knowing no one else would ever do for me. All I wanted was Kalei. Her smiles in the morning. Her touch at midday. And her soul warming my bed at night.

This female's embrace—her body and everything that made up her—would haunt me for the rest of my days.

There was nothing to do about it except tell her I wanted her as my mate.

My cock throbbed, still twitching inside her.

Keeping us locked together, I dropped to the soft soil and held her. I kissed the top of her head, cursing that I was so big and tall, because I wanted to kiss her lips, to drink of her lingering pleasure.

"I feel bad for monopolizing all your time this evening," she said, drawing a circle around one of my nipples then the other three.

"I cannot complain." I said it solemnly, but my hearts had essentially sprouted wings. They flew above the forest. It flew among the stars.

She chuckled. "Neither can I."

We laid together, eventually pulling apart, but only so she could lay beside me and stare at the stars.

"We traveled through them," she said. "Both you and me. To journey to the colony to start a new life, and then here to find each other." She snuggled closer. "We came to the colony from vastly different worlds, but we all want the same thing. A home. A family. Someone to love us for who we are, not what we look like on the outside or what we can give them. It's not about material things at all but the soul."

I hadn't looked at it that way, but she was right.

"Despite our outer differences, inside, we are the same," I said in awe. "You are like me. You want a new life and someone to love."

"I think . . ." She shook her head. "Maybe I shouldn't say this, but I love you, Forje."

I tightened my arms around her, never wanting to let go. "I feel the same."

Her breath caught.

Love filled me to overflowing. Kalei had been everything I could dream of from the moment I met her. Having the chance to talk with her, play bungafleer with her, and love her like this, made me complete. I was made up of uneven edges before I met her, and she smoothed them. She polished them and made them gleam. I was a better male solely by having her in my life.

Her belly rumbled, and she laughed. "You're starving me, Forje."

"Then I should do something about that, correct?"

"Correct."

We rose and dressed, then walked slowly back through the forest.

Soon, we'd leave the space station and go home.

Home? Not completely. The wellire I'd planted and

nurtured had been home, but now I could only picture me and Kalei at my farm. We'd finish it together and cherish it for the rest of our lives. We'd build a future where we worked the land together and brought things to life.

Another dream . . . Or was it?

No longer.

We held hands as we took the paths leading to the ballroom, not coming across Shardeene. I'd have to make time to speak with her. I wanted to tell her it didn't matter what she had to say to me because I was moving forward with Kalei.

When we went inside, we strode up to the buffet table and filled plates. I spied a selection of my favorite dishes, though they'd provided some dishes that humans and other species enjoyed as well.

"Mini weenies?" Kalei crowed, pointing. "Oh, yum." She added some of the tiny "weelies" onto her plate, and I did the same. I wasn't sure I'd enjoy them but if she did, I was more than willing to give them a try. "Oh, bread. You know bread is a carb. Its sole purpose in life is to carry butter."

"I had not heard that," I said with a laugh. Around Kalei, all I wanted to do was grin. I suspected I'd smile every day of my life if she was a part of it. Because she did, I added a big slice of bread to my plate and slathered it with butter. I'd put butter on my vegetables before, but never tried it on bread. No time like the present.

We settled at a table out on the trylar balcony, sitting among others enjoying food and the balmy evening. The station's environment was carefully controlled, but humidity rose from the plants around us, and I savored the weight of it in my lungs.

We dug into our meals with hearty appetites, and it

wasn't until the human security guard, Charlie, appeared at our table that I set down my eating implement.

"I'm sorry for interrupting," she said, shooting me an odd glance that made the tiny spikes on my spine stiffen. "I understand you're a military commander."

I nodded.

"We, um." She grumbled. "I never like to bother guests, but some of my crew are sick, and we're short staffed."

"What do you need?" I asked, my belly tightening.

"Just someone else to come with me when I confront a bunch of Vessars who've decided to crash the party."

Crash . . .? I wasn't sure what she meant, but I knew of the lizard mafia. Their tendrils reached throughout the galaxy, even to the planet where my people settled.

They'd played a role in settling the Twarvians near our colony, and from my most recent encounter, it was clear they'd continued their alliance with the Twarvians. I'd long suspected they were using the Twarvians to mine for precious jewels deep beneath the ground. The Twarvians could ooze into almost any opening, no matter how small.

When the Twarvians arrived on the planet, we'd wanted to place them far from us, but the Vessars intervened, stating the creatures were best suited to the mountainous region beyond the colony.

With the Twarvians an ongoing threat, we needed to move them, and I knew right where to place them—outside the newly constructed Vessar compound located three shuttle day's travel from the colony. Since the two got along well, they could live together.

Kalei watched us, concern in her eyes. "If you need to go, Forje, I understand."

And that was another reason to love her. This woman was the perfect mate for me. She'd understand if duty pulled me away and be there for me when I needed her, just as I would do the same for her. Together, we'd build a beautiful life together.

"Thank you," I said, scraping my chair back to stand. "I will be with you soon."

"Take all the time you need."

"I've gathered a small crew on the other side of the ballroom," Charlie said, her penetrating gaze meeting mine. "Don't take too long saying goodbye?"

The tension in her voice transmitted itself to me, making my hearts surge up into my throat. Was something bigger going on here? I'd help; I could do nothing else. But that meant leaving Kalei.

Charlie strode away, taking care to appear unconcerned, but a sharpness filled her eyes that I hadn't seen last night or this evening. She was concerned and was making me wish again I'd brought more serious weapons than a simple blade.

And because I hated to leave Kalei, the words sprang up on my tongue. I'd told myself I'd wait until tomorrow when the party ended, but I had to ask. How would she respond?

"Would you do something for me?" I asked her.

"Sure," she breathed. "What can I do?"

"Enjoy the rest of the soiree, but join me in my room after? I'm sure whatever Charlie needs won't take long."

"Of course," Kalei gushed, a ready smile rising on her face. "I already promised to be with you tonight."

"Wait in your own room, and I will come for you then."

"Yes." Her grin was wider than I'd ever seen it.

"And one other thing."

Her smile quivered before renewing, telling me that while she might not know how committed I was to her, she was willing to trust.

"I don't want anyone else but you, Kalei." I dropped to my knees beside her, though she was so tiny, this put us at eye level. "Would you be my mate, the only female I'll ever love?" I waited, not daring to breathe.

Her eyes filled with tears. "Forje. What a time to ask something like this. You have to help Charlie, but all I want to do is kiss you." Her chin lifted, and she gave me a watery smile. "Take care of what you need to do with Charlie, but know I'll be waiting for you in my room. And when you get there, I'll show you how much I want to be your mate."

CHAPTER THIRTY-SEVEN

KALEI

He wanted to mate with me! Me—Kalei—not Shardeene or anyone else.

I ate a bit more, but when I stood to get rid of our plates, Shardeene sashayed over to me.

My lips tight, I braced myself for whatever she might say.

She dropped into Forje's chair and stared at me with such an earnest gaze, I almost believed she had a bit of sweetness inside. "I want to kindly ask something of you."

I lifted my eyebrows and girded myself, pretty sure where she was going to take this.

"A yaro ago, I made a terrible mistake," she said.

"You did."

Her growl slipped out, breaking her pretty façade. "Forje loves me, and he wishes to be with me. He was going to ask me to be his mate. He still will, but you are in the way."

"Interesting story, but the ending turns out differently." I couldn't hold back my grin. "He just asked *me* to be his mate."

Her breath caught and true pain flashed in her eyes. Her shoulders curled forward before she stiffened her spine. "I did not truly want him anyway. Why would I wish to mate with a farmer who composes awful poetry?"

"His poetry is sweet, and it comes from the heart. I'm sorry you couldn't see that like I do. And I love the idea of settling on a farm with him."

"Then I wish you the best."

That, I doubted.

With a huff, she stood, and while anger flashed on her face, her hands trembled slightly. If I hadn't been looking, I wouldn't have seen it. "There are many other males in the galaxy. Many who would be eager to mate with me."

"I'm sure there are," I said, softening my tone. For one minue, she'd been in pain, and I wasn't mean. I would be devastated if I wanted Forje and waited too long to tell him. What we had was growing stronger, and it would only get better. "Good luck."

She studied my face before nodding curtly. "Thank you."

I watched as she strode back into the ballroom, her gait just a bit uneven. She'd waited too long, and she knew it. He'd moved past her and found someone new. I hoped she did the same. She could patch up her heart and find someone who'd love her as much as Forje did me.

Funny how I could believe that now. My confidence in him—and myself—was complete, and nothing was going to shake it.

With confidence in my stride for the first time in I didn't know how long, I entered the ballroom. People danced, while others queued the bar or stood along the side of the big room, sipping drinks.

Charlie and Forje must've stopped the unruly Vessars.

They hadn't made an appearance to destroy the upbeat mood.

Couples were forming, and I swore I could feel love in the air. Maybe the Match-Mating Soiree wasn't such a bad idea since it had nudged me and Forje together.

I crossed the room, smiling at anyone who looked my way, and exited through the main doors.

Despite not remembering exactly where my room was, I found it. Inside, I decided to get out of my dress and put on something sexy.

I didn't bring anything like that, but the small fabricator on the shelf inside the cleansing unit showcased a large selection. I scrolled through the choices flashing on the screen, finally selecting something pretty but—ha ha—crotchless. Who needed a crotch when Forje was around?

After selecting my outfit, I stepped into the cleansing unit. While it didn't use water, it still eliminated all dead skin cells and anything that might produce odors. I stood as the emollient spray coated my body and the driers blasted me with warm air.

When I stepped outside, I was clean and dry and ready to dress in the cute outfit I'd selected. I opened the fabricator and tugged it out, holding it up to make sure it would do.

"Perfect." It didn't take long to dress because there wasn't much to it.

I lounged on the bed, posing, then started to feel chilly. Tugging the blanket over me helped, but it ruined the sexy effect I was aiming for.

I sat in a chair but was just as cold there. A few taps on my wrist com turned up the heat, and I was soon toasty.

Maybe I should lean against the wall? I did so.

I used the evacuation unit.

I returned to my bedroom, but Forje still hadn't arrived. Worry skipped up my spine. Charlie had seemed concerned but not overly so. My assumption was a few rowdy Vessars had tried to force their way into the soiree and Charlie needed backup to convince them they'd made a mistake. They'd leave, and that would be it.

Perhaps Forje had been waylaid by Shardeene? If he had, he would've shrugged her off by now. If nothing else, I had confidence in us. I wouldn't start thinking he'd change his mind and chase after her, not when he asked me to be his mate.

I had risen from the chair, intending to lay down on the bed again, when the door hummed, telling me someone waited outside.

Yay, Forje. My blood pounded through my veins as I slid off the bed and skipped to the door.

I bypassed the lock and pressed the button to open the panel, a smile rising on my face.

Confusion swamped me, and my smile faded, replaced with the grim realization I was in trouble.

Rich stood in the hall flanked by two leering Vessar lizard guys. What was he doing with the mafia?

"Darling," Rich said with a slick smile. His smarmy gaze drifted down my body, and a shiver ripped through my veins. "So nice of you to dress like that for me."

CHAPTER THIRTY-EIGHT

FORJE

"I'm sorry I had to take you away from your date," Charlie said, hurrying down the hall. She stopped at a door marked Service and unlocked it, stepping inside.

I followed. "We won't be long, correct?"

"Well, yeah, that's the problem, you see." She handed me a zapper, a sword, and a gun belt. "Put this on."

While she rifled through a bin of laser pistols, I strapped on the belt.

"Tell me what is going on."

"See, my crew was called away."

I frowned, the spikes on my brow ridge stiffening. "Why?"

"A disturbance in the lower level."

I didn't like where this was going. "What kind of disturbance?"

"It should've been nothing."

I waited while she strapped weapons on her waist, adding a blade beneath the leg of her pants. She was taller than Kalei and had the same curvy shape. The stern look in her eyes would put most males off, but I could tell she was worried. I supposed she was attractive, with her amber hair in a snug arrangement on the back of her neck, though I wasn't sure why I noted anything about her appearance.

"The thing is, my crew didn't come back and my com has remained silent," she lifted her wrist, displaying her communicator. The symbol on the black band indicated it was a high-security device, not the standard fare most wore. "I only got one message from them saying that the Vessars were planning to storm the soiree."

"Why?"

She shrugged. "No clue."

Something was missing from this, but I couldn't figure out what it might be.

"When they didn't respond, I hailed the bridge, but they're overwhelmed with a moolee problem and couldn't send back-up. They didn't seem concerned, but I am, so I found you." She exited the weapon's closet, stopping in the hall while I joined her. "We need to discover what's going on before something horrible happens."

"What's their goal here?"

"I don't know, but I think we might find some answers in the Nessalon Hangar."

"Why there in particular?"

Her heavy glance fell on my face. "That's where the Vessars docked." Turning, she jogged down the hall, and I followed.

The station was surprisingly quiet tonight, but it was late. We didn't encounter anyone as we hurried through the corridors, which was just as well. As a jogging army, we'd scare anyone we ran into.

We continued down a new corridor on the hangar level. Charlie stopped at the end, holding up her hand, and peered carefully into the next hall. I waited, listening, but not hearing anything other than the shuffle of boots on the tile floor.

She eased back and leaned against the wall beside me, lifting her wrist. "I'm going to tell the bridge I need back-up. I apologize. I thought this would be two, three Vessars tops, but it looks like something bad is about to go down at the hangar."

"What did you see?" I asked quietly, not eager to draw the attention of what sounded like a big group of lizards waiting around the corner.

"Four guards outside the hangar, though no movement beyond the glass."

"That doesn't sound suspicious. Maybe they are preparing to depart?" It could be nothing, though unease made my spine spikes quiver, and I'd learned not to ignore the feeling.

"They're fully armed."

"So are we."

Her lips thinned. "You know station rules. No weapons on board without clearance from the bridge. Vessars never get clearance. No, they're planning something, and I need to stop whatever it is before it's too late."

Her sharp gaze met mine. Blue eyes. Unusual for my species, though it could be normal for humans. They couldn't compare to Kalei's pretty brown eyes, but I realized Charlie was attractive. And savvy. She was right about the Vessars, plus the uneasy feeling we shared.

I liked her, and I had a feeling she'd make a good friend.

She spoke quietly into her com, frowning at the reply. Her perturbed gaze met mine. "They're saying they can't spare any because of the moolees."

The pests could eat through the outer casing of a propulsion module within a horus.

"What would you like to do?" I wasn't opposed to combat if it was needed, but I wasn't sure it was in this situation. Perhaps they'd somehow obtained permission to arm themselves.

No, that couldn't be right. They were barely tolerated on the space station. Something was happening, and we needed to figure it out.

"We can go ask them what they're doing," I said.

"All right."

It shouldn't take long to question them. Then I could go to Kalei's quarters and take a step into the life I'd been dreaming of since I met her.

We rounded the corner and strode boldly up to the Vessars who fingered the hilts of weapons at their sides, though they didn't pull them from the sheaths on their sides.

"Have time for a few questions, guys?" Charlie asked pleasantly.

One grunted. The others studied me.

"What's your purpose on the space station?" she asked, her hand on her own weapon.

A standoff, then.

I remained behind and to the side of her where I could provide backup if needed.

"Go awaysss," one of the Vessars said. He quivered, and blue scales drifted from his body. They shed continually, and I couldn't imagine what their bedsheets must look like in the morning. "Not yousss businessss."

"Do you have permission to be armed?" Charlie asked.

"Go awayssss," the guard said again, his gaze meeting that of the others. "Or we makessss."

"I've called the bridge. You're not supposed to be armed," she said.

"We leavesss soon. *Yousss* leavesss now."

The guard stepped toward her.

Tension spiked up my spine.

"Back off," I growled.

The Vessars leaped, one taking me down to the floor while two grappled with Charlie. Her weapon drawn quickly, she got off a shot, hitting one in the chest. He slumped to the ground, unconscious. The other two grabbed her arms.

I bucked the one attacking me off, sending him flying into the wall. He crashed hard and slumped on the tile floor, his gaze dazed.

I scrambled toward Charlie, ripping one of the Vessars off her while kicking out at the other. He tumbled to the floor and skidded, pulling his weapon.

Charlie rolled and came up to a crouch while I punched the Vessar trying to strangle me. His nose crunched, and he bellowed as Charlie shot the fourth.

Within a secunda, we had them stunned and bound on the floor.

Charlie reported to the bridge, and they said they'd pull someone from the moolee problem and send them to take the Vessars to the brig.

She ended the call and squatted beside the only Vessar vaguely awake, pressing her weapon against his temple. "Tell me what's going on."

He hissed, saying nothing else.

She grumbled, but what could she do? "I'm sure those in the brig will be able to get more out of them." Her gaze fell on me. "Thanks for the backup. I'm sorry I had to ask."

"I'm always happy to help."

"I should be okay until the detail arrives to lock these guys up." She nudged the shoulder of one of them with the toe of her boot before turning to lean against the wall. I noted she kept her weapon in hand.

"I can stay with you."

"You had a date, right?"

Now that the tension had left the air, I could grin. "I do."

Charlie smiled, transforming her face into that of a beautiful woman. She didn't make my hearts spark like Kalei did, but that look would do it for another one dia. "Go to her. Tell her I'm sorry. And I hope you have a great evening."

With a nod, I turned and jogged toward Kalei's room.

CHAPTER THIRTY-NINE

KALEI

Pivoting on my heel, I bolted for the cleansing unit, but Rich grabbed me before I made it halfway.

"Not so fast," he hissed in my ear. "I'm not quite through with you yet."

"I don't want to be with you. We broke up ages ago. Let me go!"

"You may have divorced me, but I want more." He whipped me around and shoved me.

I stumbled toward the door, tripping. I would've fallen if the blue-skinned lizard guys with Rich hadn't grabbed me.

The lizard guy from the elevator hauled me up off my feet, dangling me so our gazes were level. "Wantssss."

"Not until I'm done," Rich said, striding past the Vessar. "Bring her. We need to get out of here before her lover returns."

"Killsss," the lizard said, lowering my feet to the floor.

I kicked out, hitting his shin, but he didn't flinch. Scales drifted to the floor like in the elevator. Did they shed all the time?

He latched onto my wrist and hauled me out through the door, wrenching it shut behind him.

As he followed Rich, I expected us to run into someone, and while I wouldn't want to endanger a passerby, I needed help. But I saw no one, maybe because they took a service route with dingy walls and muted lights overhead.

We arrived at a hangar, and I wrenched free from the lizard guy, running back the way we'd come with my bare feet slapping the tiles.

"Get her, Groxl," Rich barked. "I paid you enough to keep her from escaping."

Groxl scampered after me, his big scaly feet with two-inch claws and long legs giving him the advantage. He grabbed me and purposefully flung himself to the floor, skidding along with me lying on his chest.

"Likesss," he hissed, his hands groping me.

I squirmed, kicking and screaming, trying to break free.

His claws dug into my back, pinching the skin. "Stopsss or I takesss now."

I stilled, looking up at him through my tangled hair. "Don't do this," I whispered. "I can pay you more than Rich."

"I headsss Vessarsss. Takesss what I pleasesss."

He was the leader of the lizard mafia? "Why be Rich's lackey, then?"

Groxl snarled and scrambled to his feet, holding me off the floor, pressed against his scaled chest. The scales bit into my bare skin, but I held in my wince.

He stormed back to the hangar, stomping past Rich waiting in the opening.

"Nice catch, Groxl," Rich said.

"Where are you taking me?" I cried, twisting and flailing against Groxl's chest.

"Where we can have fun," Rich said pleasantly. He strode across the metal platform and climbed inside the open hatch of a mid-level space cruiser. "Bring her," he snapped to Groxl. "I'll take it from here."

Trapped inside the ship with him, I'd never find a way free. I squirmed and clawed, breaking my nails, but Groxl's thick hide was impervious to any attempt to harm him. He didn't even flinch.

He stepped into the ship and put me down, keeping a tight grip on my wrist.

"Bring her in here," Rich called from a stateroom ahead. "Make sure the pilot is ready, then get off the ship. Take your lizard friends with you."

Groxl stomped down a narrow hall and into the opulent room at the back end of the ship. Staterooms often took up the lower levels while this one contained the helm for the pilot, a galley and cleansing unit—perhaps—and this room at the end where the owner would ride in splendor. Leave it to Rich to make sure he only had the best.

I wrenched my arm nearly out of the socket in an attempt to get free, but Groxl's claws dug into my flesh. He whipped me forward and released me. Momentum flung me onto the sofa lining one wall, and I landed hard on my chest beside Rich.

"Hard landing?" he asked in a mocking voice. "Let me help you onto my lap." He latched onto my arm and dragged me up onto his thighs, laying me on my chest across them. He smacked my ass. "Behave, and I'll be nice."

I bit down on his thigh hard enough his skin gave way.

He shrieked and flung me onto the floor. I smacked onto my left hip and knocked the wind from my lungs. While I lay struggling to breathe, Rich rose from the sofa to tower over me.

"Comfy?" Rich—short for Richard, but I really should've called him Dick from the start—said, straddling my chest with his legs. "I told you to behave, but maybe you enjoy it rough. That's okay. I do too."

"Fuck you," I snarled.

"Oh, I'm sure we'll get around to that soon."

"I won't submit to you."

"You won't need to."

"We hassss other plansss," Groxl said, advancing toward Rich.

Rich started to turn, but he never made it.

The Vessar lizard bit off Rich's head with one bite of his elongated jaws and vicious teeth. While my jaw dropped, and I scrambled onto my ass and backward, my back hitting the side of the sofa, Groxl tossed the head against the wall.

Rich's body toppled sideways, and I jerked my gaze away before it made impact.

Groxl's leering gaze traveled down my trembling form. "Fucksss me insteadsss."

FORJE

I paced outside Kalei's room, banging on the panel each time I passed. Fear boiled inside me. Why wasn't she answering? Even worse, why didn't she respond to my call to her wrist com?

I was preparing to kick in the panel like I had the day before when a steward entered the hall, carrying a covered tray.

"Let me into this room," I barked.

Pausing beside me, she frowned. "Doesn't your com work?"

Everything was programmed through our wrist coms, but I hadn't thought to ensure I had access to Kalei's room. Why would I need it? She'd let me in if I asked.

"It is not working." I swallowed back my snarl. "Could you please let me in?"

"Let me check with central." She lowered the tray to the floor and tapped into her com. "Hmm. It says this room belongs to a female, and I do not believe that is you." Her shoulder length pink hair flared around her, and the spikes on her exposed arms lifted. She backed up two steps. "I cannot grant you entrance to another person's room."

"She is my mate. She was going to wait for me here, but she is not responding to my knock." I struggled not to sound desperate. No, I struggled not to grab the steward's hand and use her com to gain access to the room.

"What if you are . . .?" She didn't finish, perhaps because my face must blaze with fury.

"I will back away. Would you please check the room to make sure my newly engaged mate is not lying on the floor inside, injured and unable to call out?"

The steward must've worried I'd break the door down if she didn't relent. Believing I could use the weapons I still clung to since fighting beside Charlie might've added to her decision.

"Step back farther, please, sir," she said. She waited until I put a solid distance between us before gently knocking on the door. "Excuse me. Maelam? Are you in there?" She knocked again, calling out louder. "Maelam?" Her chest heaved with a sigh. "Please remain where you are." She lifted her com. The door clicked, and she nudged it open, stepping inside. "Excuse me, Maelam?"

I couldn't wait. I rushed in behind her.

Kalei wasn't there.

"I believe you are mistaken, sir," the steward said. "She is not here waiting for you. Perhaps she decided to meet up with a different friend?"

This late at night? Besides, she didn't know anyone else here.

I jogged to the cleansing unit. The door was open, suggesting she'd recently used it, and her gown hung by the door. She'd been here, and she'd changed her clothing.

"Sir, you cannot go in there," the steward said,

following me into the tiny room. "See? She is not here, either. I am asking you to return to the hall. Please place a call to your . . . mate out there."

I stomped past her, fear tightening my throat. My hearts said something was wrong, but I couldn't determine what it was.

Until I spied blue scales lying on the tile floor.

Vessars.

At least of one of them had been inside her room. I remembered Charlie wondering why they were on the space station and armed.

Kidnapping? Earth females fetched a high price at illegal auctions. Would they be bold enough to board the station and steal someone?

The Vessars I knew would.

I ran from the room and took the halls to the Nessalon Hangar with anxiety crawling up my spine. I prayed I was wrong, that Kalei had returned to the ballroom to play a game, but I knew it wasn't true.

In my soul, I *knew* they'd taken her. It didn't matter why. I would get her back, and I would make them pay for daring to come near her.

No one stood outside the hangar; Charlie and the guys we'd subdued were gone, too.

I slowed my pace and crept up to the opening, peering through the airlock to the platform beyond.

Four Vessars stood outside a ship with an open hatch. Nothing indicated Kalei was here but it wasn't like she could leave evidence.

I passed through the open airlock and strode up to them. "I'm boarding the craft."

"Not allowsss," one said, reaching for his weapon.

Shoving past him, I stomped onto the ship. I took the

hall on the right, arriving in the back room in time to see an Earth male's head smack against the tellafon wall. The male's body toppled to the ground beside Kalei.

Kalei sat on the floor with her back to the sofa, her eyes wide and her mouth ajar. She cringed as the body slumped beside her.

The mastermind of the Vessar mafia, Groxl, stood beside Kalei, leering. "Fucksss me insteadsss," he said, baring his fangs.

"Not if I have anything to say about it," I growled, flinging myself on top of him.

CHAPTER FORTY-ONE

KALEI

"Forje," I cried, scrambling away from the guys as they smacked into the wall and landed hard on the floor. They rolled together before Groxl got free and snapped to his feet.

Forje gave chase as Groxl fled the room, taking the hall in a scrambling, furious pace.

I jumped to my feet and snatched a blanket off the back of the sofa, wrapping it around me, before running down the hall and out into the hangar.

Groxl and the lizard guys were fleeing across the open platform. They dove into the open hatch of a ship farther down, and the hatch snapped closed before Forje could reach it. He banged on the panel as the engines whined.

A boom echoed in the room, and lights flashed in a circle around a big panel high on the wall.

Sirens blared, and a mechanical voice heralded an alarm. "Outer hatch opening. Outer hatch opening. Please depart the platform immediately."

Forje raced toward the airlock, snatching me up in his arms as he passed. He barely made it inside the airlock before the door slammed shut. Placing me on my feet, he waited with me for the lights beside the hallway door to stop flashing. The panel wouldn't open until the outer hatch closed.

"You are safe," Forje said, wrapping his arms around me. "I have you. They cannot harm you, my mate. I will notify the bridge, and they will apprehend the Vessar ship."

"Groxl killed Rich," I said. "But he deserved it."

"That was the beheaded male?"

I nodded. "He was kidnapping me. He was going to force me to be with him." Goosebumps rippled across my skin. "I'm so glad you got here in time."

The outer hatch opened, and the Vessar craft shot through.

"I will always be here for you, Kalei. You are my love. My mate. The perfect female for me."

"Forje." I grinned up at him. "I love you."

"And I love you, Kalei. Where would I be if you hadn't come to the colony to domesticate me?"

"Frankly, you're perfect already. No domestication needed."

His arms tightened around me. "You are beauty. Love. And the sparkle in my life."

I hugged him, knowing a wonderful future waited for us back at the colony. "I think the first thing we need to do when we get home is to pay a visit to your—no, *our* —farm."

"There is no place I would rather take you, mate."

CHAPTER FORTY-TWO

EPILOGUE: KALEI
A FEW LUNAR CYCLES LATER

"I think we should get some turnip seeds from Earth," I said, putting my back into hoeing a line in the soft soil where we would plant yeelars.

"Yeelars are best," Forje said. He hefted a boulder he'd unearthed and carried it over to the cart. The culair hitched to it turned to watch him, huffing softly.

I was a bit startled when he introduced me to the pets he'd imported here from other planets, including a culair he adopted from an orc who raised them in a colony three cruiser days' travel from here. Kreel was the orc's name, and he'd mated with an Earthling too.

The next time Forje traveled there, I was going with him. I wasn't sure about orcs, but I craved the companion-ship of other Earth females.

"I think you'll enjoy turnips," I said, dutifully planting a yeelar. "And parsnips and carrots."

After dropping the boulder in the cart, he turned and leaned against the metal surface. "I am uncertain about these caroots."

"We need sunflowers too." Straightening, I brushed the

dirt off my hands. I looked around with satisfaction soothing my bones. Our wellire had matured, and I'd almost freaked out when Forje stepped through the outer wall—without a door in sight. He'd reappeared at my shriek and assured me this was normal, that the opening would form on its own in the place he chose after communing with the plant.

Communing with a plant . . . I wasn't sure what I thought about that, but it worked. The space he'd requested had been crafted as the plant grew, and in addition to the living area, a bedroom, a kitchen, and a cleansing unit, the mushroom had left an area for more bedrooms and even an office. Forje told me he'd work with the plant to form those rooms after we moved in.

Which we did yesterday. Newly mated, we couldn't wait for some alone time. His aunties, who I now called Auntie, too, tended to stroll into rooms unannounced . . .

But no more! We'd moved into our wellire at the farm, and next week, Forje would start a part-time consulting job with the government. No more battling Twarvians. Instead, he'd help develop systems that would keep them away from the colony without causing death to either side. The Twarvians deserved to live; we just didn't want them eating us to survive.

There was some talk of relocating them, and I hoped they were able to make the arrangements.

As for the Vessars, we hadn't seen or heard from them since Groxl's ship left the space station. The command center had tried to engage a beam to haul the cruiser back, but the Vessars broke the band and escaped.

"In addition to turnips, carrots, and parsnips, I want to grow flowers," I said. "Lots of flowers. We can sell bouquets at the market."

Forje nodded slowly before launching into verse, something he did often. Most of the time, his poems made my heart pinch tight. Other times, they were funny and made me laugh. He was contemplating submitting them to an interstellar publisher for publication. I hoped they accepted them. He'd be thrilled to hold a book full of his work in his hands.

"Caroots are tasty," he composed, his voice lifted. "Parsneeps are bland. But the great turneep is the master of them all."

I clapped. "Not bad. Not bad at—" Frowning, I stared past him. An alien guy walked toward us, and I just now noted a shuttle parked on the open field behind him. How had I missed it landing?

He was as tall and broad as Forje, though he had silvery blue skin instead of Forje's gorgeous green.

As he approached, his white hair streamed behind him. His head lifted, and his piercing blue eyes met mine. Even if he wasn't dressed in uniform, the look in his eyes would give him away.

Interstellar cop.

His hand remained on the hilt of his weapon sheathed on his hip.

He stopped a few feet away from Forje, his sharp gaze traveling back and forth between us. He didn't seem surprised to see a human female here, though I was the only one who'd settled in the colony so far.

"I hate to bother you," he said in a gruff, cultured voice. "I'm looking for Forje Traach'eol."

"*I* am Forje," my mate said.

I was surprised his fingers remained well away from his weapons he wore all the time. Maybe he saw something in this alien I didn't. Hefting the hoe, I scurried over to them, but though I was determined to protect my mate, I didn't put myself between them. Not yet.

Watch out, buddy. One wrong move, and I'll hoe you.

"I'm Shaede Chorkain," he said. "And I need to speak to you about an assignment I'm on."

Forje leaned against the cart. The culair we'd named Fred stomped his feet, but he didn't charge or breathe fire—a point in Shaede's favor.

"Could we speak alone?" Shaede asked, his hand leaving his weapon long enough to push back the hair drifting into his face.

"You may speak in front of my mate," Forje said, crossing his arms on his chest.

"All right," Shaede said easily. "I'm on a mission to recover a kidnapped female, and I heard you were one of the last to see her. I came here to find out if there were any details you hadn't shared with the space station's commander."

"Who was kidnapped?" I asked, a chill sinking into my bones.

"Charlie," he said, and for one second only, grief flashed in his eyes. He fingered a small pendant hanging from a chain around his neck before tucking it back beneath his shirt. A melancholy look appeared in his eyes, almost mournful.

That was the minue I realized this guy was handsome in a hard, rough-edges kind of way and that his heart was aching.

"You mean my friend, the security guard, Charlie?" I asked.

"Yes, Charlotte Ludgrove is an old friend, though she might not agree with me using that term."

Forje watched us, speculation in his eyes.

I frowned. "You're not friends?"

"We go way back. Her older brother is an old military buddy of mine. We trained together in the Interstellar Interpol."

I'd only vaguely heard about the organization. "You're like those ancient James Bond stories."

"Who is James Bond?" Shaede asked.

"007. You know."

He shook his head and trained his attention on Forje. "I need any information you can give me."

Forje shared the details of how we'd met, and what happened when he last saw her.

"The Vessars took her?" I asked, my knees shaking. It had been nearly two weeks. She'd been their captive that long? I remembered the leer in Groxl's eyes. He hadn't hurt her, had he?

My guts on fire, I went over to lean against Forje.

"Intel suggests she's on the prison planet, and I'm going to get her back," Shaede said grimly. "If I have to take down the entire compound to do it, I will."

I wouldn't want to be in his path while he did it.

"Is there anything else you remember?" Shaede asked Forje with quiet desperation. "Even a tiny detail could make a difference."

"I am sorry," Forje said. "That is it."

"Do you know anything about the prison planet?" he asked.

"Not much. I have not been there," Forje said. "No one has. It will be a challenge for you to get past the outer wall."

Shadows drifted through Shaede's eyes. "I have no choice."

"Everyone has a choice," Forje said.

"I not only owe her brother, but I also owe Charlie," Shaede said. "I . . . made a mistake."

What kind of mistake? Was there something between them other than possible friendship?

"You think rescuing her will even things out?" I asked, curious. What had he done?

"That's what I'm going to find out." He tapped his forehead with a claw. "Thanks. I'll let you two return to your gardening." He turned and walked slowly back to the shuttle. The tightness of his shoulders was belied by the aura of sadness lingering around him.

"I hope she's okay," I said, upset I hadn't noticed she was gone.

"I have a feeling Shaede will make sure of that," Forje said, his arms going around me.

He held me for a long while, both of us grateful we were safe and had each other but fearful for Charlie.

I turned and looked up at him, my eyes stinging with tears and my lips trembling.

"She will be all right," he said, smoothing the hair from my face.

I nodded.

We had hope that the government would keep the Twarvians away, but what would hold back the Vessars?

The might of Forje and guys like Shaede, I assumed. I'd have to trust they'd keep the colony safe.

"It is time," Auntie Rozen called from the door to our wellire.

"Time for what?" Forje asked.

Aunt Enzia joined Rozen at the door, putting her arm around her sister. "You know very well what it is time for. We have labored all day to craft this special treat, and you must come inside to taste it."

"Well said, sister," Rozen said. "Well said."

Enzia gave us all a pert nod. "Thank you."

"You do know that I did most of the work, however," Rozen added.

Enzia poked Rozen's side. "That is incorrect, sister. *I* did most of the work while you moaned and complained, reclining on the sofa."

"How dare you?" Rozen gaped at her sister. "*I* did most of the work, and you know it!"

Enzia winked at us and scooted back inside the wellire, calling out as she started up the stairs. "Do come in and taste my creation!"

"That female," Rozen growled. "*Her* creation? How dare she?" She scurried inside. "Sister. Sister!" Her voice faded as the mushroom stem's door panel slid shut.

"Well," I said.

"Well, is correct," Forje said.

"Do we dare go inside?"

"I do not believe we have much choice."

"I suppose you're right."

He lifted me off my feet for a heady kiss that soon got me moaning. Maybe we could sneak away after tasting whatever it was that they'd created. It had been hours since we were together, and I needed my mate.

I leaned back in his arms and grinned, about to make the suggestion.

"Do not dawdle," Enzia called from an upper window. "If you do not hurry, Rozen will eat the entire treat."

Forje and I looked at each other and burst into laughter.

I hope you enjoyed Forje & Kalei's story

as much as I enjoyed writing it.
Would you like another peek at them
living happily together?
Sign up for my newsletter
& receive a free bonus scene!

Next in the Series is
Handcuffing the Alien.
Scroll forward for Chapter 1 . . .

ABOUT THE AUTHOR

Ava Ross is a two-time *USA Today* Bestselling author who has written numerous titles, all of them featuring sweet and steamy romance. She fell for men with unusual features when she first watched Star Wars, where alien creatures have gone mainstream. She lives in New England with her husband (who is sadly not an alien, though he is still cute in his own way), her kids, and a few assorted pets.

SERIES BY AVA

Mail-Order Brides of Crakair

Brides of Driegon

Fated Mates of the Ferlaern Warriors

Fated Mates of the Xilan Warriors

Holiday with a Cu'zod Warrior

Galaxy Games

Alien Warrior Abandoned/
Shattered Galaxies

Beastly Alien Boss

Bride of the Fae

Stranded With an Alien/A Sci-fi Holiday Tail

Monsterville, USA
(Includes Monster Between the Sheets
& Sweet Monster Treats)

You can find my books on Amazon.

HANDCUFFING THE ALIEN

My alien hero not only wants to rescue me, but he also wants to claim me too.

Wrongfully convicted of murder and sentenced to hard labor on an alien prison planet, I think my life is over. Until my rescue comes in the form of my older brother's best friend, Shaede—a blue-skinned alien who broke my heart years ago. But he gets caught too, and before you know it, we're handcuffed together and locked in a cell with only one bunk.

Shaede is determined to save us, no matter the cost. And in the meantime, he plans to convince me that he made a big mistake turning me down . . . and he wants to claim me as his.

Handcuffing the Alien is Book 6 in the Beastly Alien Boss Series. Each book is loosely connected and features an Earth woman hired for an off-world job who meets a gruff alien who can't resist falling for his fated mate.

Get your copy NOW!

CHAPTER 1
CHARLIE

"See the galaxies," the Interstellar Employment Agency employee told me. "Enjoy new foods and meet exciting alien people!"

I doubted the guy at the Agency had a Vassar jail in mind when he said that. Neither did I.

I'd just been laid off by Interstellar Interpol, so when the opportunity to travel to the Plushier Space Station to provide security for a Match-Mating Soiree came up, I jumped. It wasn't my usual kind of assignment. Who expected to make a drug bust during a matchmaking event?

But a recent split with a decent guy who just wasn't right gave me the extra push I needed to take the job. He was one in a long string of guys who also weren't "right" thanks to my teenage crush, Shaede, who stomped all over my heart. He made me see any guy I'd met since then was not quite enough.

There was nothing wrong with a woman pining for an alien hottie who turned her down, correct?

Okay, so it *had* been six years, but the pinch still thrived in my heart.

If the alien lizard mafia, the Vessars, hadn't tried to infiltrate the Soiree, and I hadn't knocked a bunch of them out, they wouldn't have kidnapped me and sent me to their prison planet.

It was funny how one simple move could take a woman's life in a completely different direction.

And now, here I was, sneaking around the prison while everyone else slept.

As I stood in the hall between the long row of prison cells, I hitched my wig lower on my forehead. A quick swipe of my finger told me my auburn tresses weren't peeking out from beneath the fake hair. A glance down told me my uniform looked like everyone else's and that my boobs remained bound beneath the snug cloth encircling my chest.

In case any of my fellow inmates were watching, I made sure my pace resembled that of a guy. I thanked all that was fated that the warden and my fellow inmates hadn't seen past the disguise I donned while locked inside the hold of the Vessar ship that brought me here. Everyone thought I was a teenage boy. It paid to keep a wig and binder on your person at all times.

Maybe my boss shouldn't have been so hasty in laying me off. Look at me, working for free on the case he'd quashed, stating we'd never figure out what the Vessars were up to on their prison planet.

Tonight, I'd completed another reconnaissance mission that went nowhere, so maybe my boss hadn't been that far off in his assumption this case was dead.

A niggling feeling in the middle of my spine—the area that still ached from when I jumped a hornburr on Quixan 5 and he fought back—told me something odd was going on here. If only I could figure it out. I'd snuck out of my cell to search the areas of the compound I could reach as often as I could during the lunar cycle I'd been incarcerated here, but I hadn't found much to build a case on.

My cell door gave way with a subtle creak when I pushed it open, making me freeze and peer around.

A soft cheep echoed behind me, and I jumped. Turning, I scooped Rosie up from the stone floor. I'd befriended the rodent-like creature within a dia of arriving here. She'd popped out from beneath my bunk and climbed onto my chest. I assumed she'd been tamed by whoever occupied the cell before me.

The whiskers on the tip of her long nose twitched, and her long tail coiled around my wrist, holding tight.

I stroked her fluffy pale blue fur and listened.

When no one called out, I slipped inside my cell and pulled the barred door shut. My heart stalled when the lock clicked into place, and I worried my lower lip with my teeth, wondering if I'd have time to discover the warden's plan before my guise was discovered.

With a grunt, I kicked off my boots and sank onto my hard bunk, lowering Rosie to my side. She coiled close to my warmth and sighed. I dragged the scratchy blanket over us and rubbed my face with my palms. There was nothing I could do but continue this mission.

When I disarmed the Vessars on the space station during the Match-Mating Soiree, I never thought they'd grab me. They'd tossed me into the hold of their ship, where I quickly donned my disguise. Other Vessars brought me to the prison planet, where they put me through a hasty trial where I wasn't given the chance to defend myself. A grainy vid showed me "assaulting" the Vessars, and that was all the "jury" of angry lizards needed.

I was sentenced to one yaro hard labor that would've been served on my back if they realized I was female.

Like all the other able-bodied inmates, they sent me to work in the mines.

If I were lucky, I'd continue to provide them with what they sought over everything else until I'd gathered enough information and could flee. I worried I wouldn't be able to keep them satisfied with my haul since they *really* loved what I retrieved from beneath the planet's surface.

After tossing and turning for a while, I gave up on sleeping and stared at the ceiling. Rosie's soft snores erupted from beside me, and I stroked her fur, grateful I had her as a friend.

The barred narrow window mounted in the stone wall on my left let in a slip of dawn. Guards would be here soon to escort me to my next day at work.

I tossed my holey blanket to the side and slid off the bunk, covering Rosie so she could keep sleeping. I crossed to the wall near the foot of my bed and made a careful mark in a stone slab. Thirty-one. Only three-hundred and thirty-four dias left in my sentence.

Yeah, I'd escape long before that.

I should crawl back onto my bunk and suck in the bit of heat I'd left behind, but all I could think of was what I would attempt soon. I'd searched most of the main prison building and a few of the nearby structures, and it was time to check out the rest of the compound. Unfortunately, I'd be in full view of the guards at the top of the wall when I crossed the open areas between here and the buildings.

Pacing the tiny space, my bare feet silent on the stone floor, I ticked everything on my list for the thousandth time. Once I'd discovered the prison's secrets, I'd have to flee.

Food and water were hidden away.

Both had come at some expense to my body, but it should be enough to get me across the wasteland surrounding the prison. Once I'd reached the other side, I'd find a way off this forsaken planet. Then, I'd beat down my former boss's door and show him the evidence I'd worked hard to obtain—assuming I could obtain it.

I'd send reinforcements to free my fellow prisoners.

Would the credits I'd gained in trades with the guards be enough to buy my passage off the planet? Maybe I should trade for a few more.

I'd already hidden a sack of clothing with everything else.

What else did I need? I'd spent every waking moment going through my final escape plan until it felt seamless, but there were so many unknown variables that might trip me up.

What if I—

Footsteps whispered in the hall.

I fled to my bunk. Only the shift of the blanket betrayed me as I tucked myself in beside Rosie.

I punctured the dawn with a low groan and muttered something incomprehensible to add to the impression I was having a nightmare. There was nothing new about that. My dreams had been haunted by images of someone grabbing me while I mined and realizing there was a female hidden beneath my dirty clothing.

If the vein of brugeer I'd discovered ran out and I didn't find another, they might send me to a different mine to work. Then I'd have to start all over again, hiding food, water, and whatever else I'd need to escape across the wasteland.

Only the brugeer kept me safe. That and one of the

inmates watching out for me. He said I reminded him of his little brother, which made me laugh inside.

Turning, I faced the door to my cell. It was still dark enough that whoever approached would think me asleep, even with my eyes slitted. A person could never be too careful, especially with lizard aliens.

The footsteps came closer, and the person paused outside my cell, watching me. When a series of low clicks rang out, I tensed.

"Charlie," a male voice whispered, his face hidden in shadows.

Tall. Bulky. Maybe bluish skin. He wasn't one of my fellow lizard prisoners or a guard.

Tension spiked through me. I didn't like change.

"Charlie? Shit, are you dead?" Desperation came through in the guy's voice.

My breath caught.

No, no, no.

It couldn't be *him*.

It had been six yaros. I had to be mistaken.

Shaede Dil'in Chorkain couldn't be standing on the other side of my cell door.

"Go away," I snarled.

Really lame there, Charlie, the voice on my right shoulder —my conscience—said.*Really lame.*

She's wise, the voice on my left shoulder—my snarky side—said.

When a girl was locked up for over a month, she had to talk to someone other than a fluffy blue rodent.

"Is that how you treat your rescuer?" The cocky self-confidence in the guy's voice had been branded into my skin yaros ago.

Back then, I'd been a newly minted eighteen-year-old

to his twenty-four, but me finally being legal hadn't made me appealing enough for a hot-shot interstellar agent like him.

"I said go away." I had to be dreaming. No, it was a true nightmare.

"Get out of bed, Charlie. I'm getting your ass out of here."

The last time I'd heard that cultured voice, the same snideness had come through in his oh-so-polite but just as devastating rejection.

Light grew in the cell, revealing he hadn't changed a bit since I last saw him.

I skimmed my gaze down his tall, broad body, taking in the new scar on his silvery blue face. I hoped to find flaws that would make it easier to forget how I threw myself at him only for him to tell me I was too young. Too innocent. Too unappealing. He hadn't outright named the last, but it had come through loud and clear in his voice.

He shoved back a strand of his white hair, revealing piercing blue eyes that had caught and held me the minue I met him—when my older brother brought home the best friend he'd met at interstellar cop training.

An alien as well, Matis wasn't my blood brother, but he took me under his wing when I was five to his fourteen. He'd protected me from the other kids at the orphanage, and we'd been close ever since.

When I met Shaede, I was seventeen and still living at the orphanage. Back then, my eyes were full of stars after the tales Matis shared about spaceships and danger. I'd seen Shaede as a hero just like the brother I looked up to. A warrior. Someone I could fall in love with.

He'd generated a galaxy of dreams for my poor little heart. Until he stomped those dreams into the ground.

"At least you're not dead." He cleared his throat and kept his tone low. Wise on his part. The guys around me slept lightly. One never knew what might creep up on you while you slumbered. "I'm here to rescue you."

"I'm not ready to leave yet," I hissed. Despite wanting to turn my back on him and pretend he didn't exist, I flicked back the blanket and sat on the edge of my bunk.

Rosie hopped onto the floor and scurried beneath, hiding.

Shaede lounged against the bars. "That makes absolutely no sense. Put your boots on and step in line, soldier."

"You're not my boss."

"Same thing."

"Not even close."

"*I'm* in charge of this mission."

"Not as far as *I'm* concerned."

"I'm not going to argue with you about it. Matis sent word you were here, and I've come to rescue you."

"Where is Matis?" I'd expected my brother to find a way to free me, not asked Shaede to do it for him.

"He's . . . not available."

On a mission, then.

"That's why you've got me," Shaede added.

Interesting way of phrasing it. If only my silly heart didn't flop around at the thought of "having" Shaede.

"I don't need you." Want and need were two different things, and I could keep the first from snatching control and running away with my soul. I was no longer eighteen and innocent. As for unappealing, there wasn't much a woman could do about something like that, especially while wearing a black wig and chest binder.

Who the hell cared what Shaede thought about me? I

hated that the hard shell around my heart might still have a crack wide enough for him to creep back inside.

"When I'm ready to leave, I'll get out of here on my own," I said.

"You're locked in a cell." His cocky chuckle rang out.

"Don't laugh. And I'm not locked in."

"Not laughing. And you are."

It was his smirk that made me want to snarl, the same one he'd displayed six yaros ago when he shot me down. Fury blazed across my soul.

He gripped the bars, and I noted a pack slouched by his feet. "You want out or not?"

Even if I needed help, he'd be the last one I'd hand my fate to.

"You need to leave," I said, hopping off the bunk and stuffing my feet into my boots. "I'll be along eventually."

His gaze traveled down my frame in a way it hadn't six yaros ago.

Like one glance from Shaede could hit a switch no one else had discovered, my veins pulsed madly. I wore grubby clothing and a wig. My boobs were compressed against my chest. The curves I'd enjoyed had shriveled because there wasn't much to eat here. How his gaze could hold admiration was beyond me.

"Don't look at me that way," I said, wishing my voice came out stronger.

"You've changed, Charlie."

"Time does that to a person."

Frowning, he stabbed his fingers through his hair. It was a wonder he didn't slice it all off with his thumb claw. "You look—"

Shouts rang out in the hall, and dismay widened his eyes.

Adrenaline spiked my pulse into overdrive. My palms became clammy.

"Great," I snapped. "You need to hide, Shaede."

He shoved open the door, grabbed my hand, and hustled me into the hall. "Just stay behind me."

I'd never remain behind any male, not even a hot one like him.

Two guards rushed toward us, and a glance over my shoulder showed five more coming from the opposite direction. I could handle two alone. Seven might present a challenge.

"Maybe you should remain behind me," I said, shouldering past him to run toward the closest guards.

I'd intended to slink across the wasteland once I'd figured out what was going on here, not stomp my way out with my fists. Leave it to Shaede to decide my fate once again.

Shaede spun to challenge the guys coming from the other direction, his thick horns slicking through the air. As I swept one of the guard's feet out from beneath him and landed a solid hit to the other's solar plexus, I caught Shaede leaping, barreling into the other guards like a ball hitting pins. They tangled together and crashed to the stone floor.

My fellow inmates clung to the bars of their cells, most watching silently, a few cheering me and Shaede on. None rooted for the guards.

"What you doing?" My friend, Pralk, asked from his cell, concern lighting up his voice.

I didn't have time to reply.

Using my favorite move, I grabbed the necks of the two I battled and brought their heads together, taking in the satisfying crack they made when they connected. The lizard aliens slumped, and I turned in time to see two guards out of commission but the other three holding Shaede down while messing up his pretty face.

I wasn't sure why I cared about them leaving bruises, except a soft feeling still lingered inside me for my older brother's best friend. I'd tried to stomp the feeling into oblivion, but a tiny flame still flickered.

"Run," he cried, struggling to break free of the guards.

I snarled and leaped toward them, hitting the chest of a particularly tall, gray skinned Vessar guard. We tumbled to the floor, but lizards were not only cunning, but they also got slippery when angry, their scaly skin secreting an oil that made them extra hard to hold on to. We grappled, but my hands kept sliding across his skin.

In no time, I lay beneath him, never a treat considering Vessar claws, pointed-tip tails, and vicious teeth.

He hauled me up as the other two wrangled with Shaede. Shaede's bellows turned to grunts that muted to silence. My guts were wrenched sideways by fear.

The Vessar dragged me across Shaede's still body. He tossed me into my cell, and I slammed against the wall above my bunk, dropping onto the equally hard surface that still held my warmth.

The guard locked my door and grabbed Shaede's bag before stomping over to the others.

I slid off the bunk, chomping my teeth on the groan eager to escape. I'd hurt my right leg when I hit the wall, but I couldn't let on that I was injured. A thing like that would be seen as weakness, and inside a prison, weakness spiraled into a quick death.

A guard hefted Shaede's leg. Shaede didn't move or respond, making me worry he was dead. My heart curled into a tight ball at the thought of a galaxy without him.

He'd devastated me six yaros ago. He didn't deserve a speck of my pity, let alone something bordering close to affection.

While the inmates around me slunk back to their bunks, the guards stomped down the hall, dragging Shaede across the stone floor behind them.

Pick up your copy of Handcuffing the Alien NOW!